*****

O, the suffering, the sweet suffering.

Come to me and cleanse the filth out of my soul.

Purify me with your whip and lick my wounds with your venom.

Only through you will the Sun shine upon the truth.

Only through you will the strength to cast evil embrace me.

O, the suffering, the sweet suffering...

How terrible and beautiful you are...

Darkborn Messiah, Tyler Nomax

Published in June 2022

ISBN: 9798837685828

TYLER NOMAX

DARKBORN MESSIAH

Whoever is reading these lines,
This book is dedicated to you…

T.N.

Contents

CHAPTER 1 - MISERIAE
CHAPTER 2 - LEGIO
CHAPTER 3 - BEATI QUI SUFFERUNT
CHAPTER 4 - PERSONAE NON GARTAE
CHAPTER 5 - NOVO MODO
CHAPTER 6 - TUUM ARBITRIUM

CHAPTER 1
MISERIAE

How did it come to this? thought William, his tongue circling the small metal tube.

How the hell did it come to this? How? Is this what I wanted? Is this what I dreamt about every night? Then why am I shaking? he asked himself, wondering how it would taste if licked. It was sour, as expected. But there was something else there. Something completely unexpected: a hint of mint.

It was almost laughable: wondering in his current predicament how that piece of metal came to taste of mint. Then he remembered. A bitter smile spread on his face.

"Go ahead; you deserve it," said the man standing behind him.

All William could manage was a few vowels. His tongue pressed the metal tube up onto his palate.

"Go ahead; you've paid your dues; you don't owe anyone anything. Do it; spare yourself. You've suffered enough," whispered the man in his right ear now.

When did it come to this? thought William, *Just this morning, I was in my warm bed, playing with my children, sipping my Columbian coffee. How the fuck is there a gun in my mouth now?*

"Get on with it! You know the alternative. You really

think you could take it? Do it, spare yourself!" William's eardrums hurt; the shout was so loud.

For a split second, his brain ordered his finger to start pulling the trigger.

How the hell did I end up with this gun in my mouth?

Only sixteen hours earlier, William Rudned had opened his eyes in his king size bed, unable to remember anything for a moment. Little did he know that knowing nothing and being lost was a gift, albeit for a moment. Ignorance was indeed bliss.

Then came that familiar, recurrent feeling. A dreadful, inexplicable blend of confusion, guilt and fear.

He'd had a wonderful dream. A dream of lust, sodomy and freedom. A wet dream. And woken up with a hard-on. He couldn't remember the last time he'd felt this way, just that he once had. He remembered his youth, the period between his childhood and teenage years. The juices rushing through his body could have been the remnant of a distant memory. A memory stuck in a cage deep beneath his soul, if there was one. A memory of ecstasy that tingled in his belly and gave him goose pimples all over. Like snuggling into a soft blanket of hope by a fireplace on a winter's night, without a single worry. But it was not to last.

Then came a thunderous realization: he was awake. The night was over, which meant that the dream was gone, along with that sweet euphoria. Reality thrashed every nerve ending in his body. He felt utterly hopeless.

It was nothing new.

William was always an odd one. Rich, handsome, intelligent, and he had a life most people could only dream of. That he could not be happy or content was unthinkable.

But he was not.

Even with all his wealth and comfort, girlfriends, popularity, and wild parties, a dark place had always skulked in his soul. Deep anger and hate enkindled by his loveless parents, who neither understood nor accepted him. An anger caused by years of systematic emotional torture. A hate that had defied all the sex, popularity and comfort.

In his parents' eyes, he was never good enough; he was either spoiled or too enthusiastic, too miserable or too demanding, too full of dreams, too naïve. Buried deep under that rarefied life of glamour, an inky sense of worthlessness stoked an unimaginable pain.

The odd part, ironically, was that despite being surrounded by all that darkness, his soul still was full of love. On his first flight as a boy, he had gazed at the sky outside the window, above the clouds, and imagined how close he was to God and Heaven. A remnant of that pure light still remained somewhere deep inside.

But the darkness lurking in his soul was much closer to the surface, and always one push away. Mighty and dark enough to consume anyone. A powerful and violent darkness that many people had gotten a taste of in his youth, causing several broken noses and black eyes. The real butchery, however, that occurred in his mind ended with far worse than mere broken bones: faces smashed into a pulp, slashed throats gushing blood splashing and severed limbs, accompanied by William's demented laughter.

His soul could well have been molded into shape by a force part angel, part devil. Absurd as it seemed, this blend was as much a gift as a curse. It was as if he were a hybrid spirit, never entirely belonging to one, yet enfolded by both.

But it was time to retrain that darkness. At the age of forty-two, he was a respected businessman now. He had been married for fourteen years to the beautiful Rachel, and they had two children: a boy and a girl. Two beautiful little people he would have given his life for without a blink. That pain no longer needed to be numbed; responsibility for his precious children had replaced the earlier wild years. He loved his family. He had reached a state of peace; not an ordinary peace, more like drugged apathy. A synthetic serenity born out of fear of losing the things he was blessed with: his family, wealth and security. Fear of offending God, if that invisible force noticed his ungrateful thoughts of debauchery and rebellion. The reality was that everything in his life floated chaotically in a loop before his eyes; he was just an observer. With little, if any, control over anything. The days, weeks, years just happened. That was all.

Yet, the beast inside had been knocking on the door, roaring louder and louder. A beast born out of fear, fed on anger, thrived in hate and laid the seeds of the darkness inside him.

His morning routine was to wake up, grab a bite, kiss his wife and children goodbye, and head off to work. At least, this was how it looked on the outside. In actual fact, he'd be questioning life, its systems and the meaning behind it all. Why would anyone bother to get out of bed and start a day identical to the previous one or the next? Was it money? Fame? Power? Sex? Maybe for some. But not for William. Not any longer. He already had it all and saw that in the end, they amounted to nothing. *How would these concepts sustain someone for a lifetime? Shouldn't there be more? Something better?* There was something growing inside him. Something terrible and beautiful.

"Hey, you little devils," said William as the children jumped onto the bed. He crossed his legs and turned his lower body to the side, hoping the erection would go away. Rachel was in the bathroom; he could hear the blow dryer.

"Dad!" shouted Charlie like he was miles away, "Look what I've done!"

The boy handed him something made of stone. It didn't look like anything at first sight. It was painted in black and resembled SS helmets from World War Two, something William was close to an expert on. It was a sickening thought: how could he liken a 12-year old's work to one of those bastards' helmets? What should have become a good memory would now always be tainted by those racists.

"Wow, cool," said William, careful to avoid subjecting his children to the constant criticism he'd grown up with. He said the first thing he could think of without hurting Charlie's feelings or crushing his self-esteem: "Looks awesome; what is it exactly? A motorcycle helmet?"

"No, Dad, it's Darth Vader!"

"Oh, the Dark Lord of the Sith! Silly me! I must be still half asleep. Well done; keep it up."

"It's for you," said Charlie, handing it over.

"Thank you, Charlie. I'll put it in my office next to the others you made. I love you, son," said William. Another thing he'd been deprived of as a child. His children wouldn't be, though; he made a point of showering them with love.

"Daddy, daddy!" Candice leapt on him, "I don't want to go to school today, daddy. Please…"

"Why's that, sweetie?" he asked.

"There's this girl at school and she makes fun of me; I hate her daddy," Candice replied.

That word made him wonder what an eight-year-old could know about hate. Had he passed it onto his children? The idea that they would inherit anything from him was intolerable. Especially the darkness.

His fond "Baby, who'd make fun of such a beautiful and sweet girl like you; she must be craazyy…" brightened Candice's sour face with that extended *craazyy*.

"She does, daddy, she does, I swear. Her name's Precious and she says my feet stink. But I wash them all the time, daddy; they don't smell, I checked," she said.

"Hmm, let me have a sniff." William grabbed her right foot, pulled it up to his face and sniffed loudly, "Oh, yeah, she's right, they do. But they smell like roses."

Candice giggled.

"And anyway, the only funny thing here's her name, Precious," he said.

They burst into laughter.

"Look baby, sometimes little girls get envious of other little girls and they try to make them feel bad. That's all. Next time she says your feet stink, you tell her that you can wash your feet but she can't wash the ugly off her face, all right?"

"William!" yelled Rachel from the doorway, "Candice, darling, don't you ever say that to anyone; it's rude. And what do we always say?"

"We should never answer badness with badness," mother and daughter said as one.

"Isn't that right, daddy?" Rachel asked William.

"Sure, baby, mommy's right. We shouldn't. I'm sorry. Just tell Precious her hair smells too," said William with a grin.

"William!" Rachel protested, suppressing a smile.

"OK, daddy, I love youuu," said Candice, running out of the room.

William envied children for their short attention span to all things nasty. *If only people could hold on to that later in life,* he thought, *the world would be so much better!*

"Get dressed, Candice, no play, we'll be late," Rachel yelled behind her.

"All right, mommy! Charlie, come on, we have to get ready; we'll be late," Candice shouted from a distance.

14

"William, you should never teach her stuff like that," Rachel said.

"OK, OK, I got you. But that little bitch deserves it, though, right?" William grinned again.

"Come on, you big baby, get up!" Rachel teased him.

"Not before I get my treat!" Catching her arm, he pulled her down to the bed.

"Will, the children…" Rachel said as he squeezed her breasts. Ignoring the objection, William gave her a long kiss. She responded by grabbing his erection under the quilt.

"All right, naughty boy, that's enough, out of bed, now!" she commanded, "And your breath smells like cigars. Take this and chew one after each smoke, please. We don't want your co-workers to gossip about your foul breath, do we?"

The small box of mints she threw missed his head by a whisker.

"Hey, be careful. And it's just leaves, nothing disgusting," he protested.

"That's what you think, darling," Rachel replied.

"OK, OK, put it in my coat pocket, please," said William, pointing to the black coat hanging on the rack.

"I will. But use them, William, I mean it. And get out of bed already," she warned him as she placed the mints in the left pocket.

"All right, I will. But first, I need my coffee."

"You know where it is; get it yourself, you lazy boy," Rachel said and left.

William was vexed. He was hoping to be served a hot cup of coffee in bed. With a grumble, he got up and headed to the hallway where the coffee machine was. He poured a cup and jumped back into the bed to sip it while browsing the morning news. The coffee half finished, he rose and headed to the shower.

The unwelcome thoughts rushed in whenever he was alone in the bathroom. While he was occupied with his children, those deep thoughts took a break. But as soon as he was alone, the search would begin again; it always ended with him sinking deeper into depression.

He had always been prone to it. He had battled obsessions all his life, accompanied by chronic depression. The worst period was between the ages of eighteen and thirty. Counting numbers, need for symmetry, order in everything, checking the oven, lights, gas, or door locks: the whole nine yards. On one occasion, he had taken his tailor ten work suits for six days in a row, just to have the hems adjusted in order to find the length that would be admired by everyone else. Up and down, up and down, half an inch up one day, one inch down the next. By the end, the hems were so frayed and his tailor so fed up that the poor fellow had refused to serve William any longer.

But the worst was the sense of uncleanness. Everything that touched something or someone had to be cleaned. If even the tip of his scarf touched the floor, it had to go to dry cleaning. If his coat came into contact with another, it too had to go. Moreover, anything that he wore, even if it was not contaminated by his standards, was a potential risk to other clothes. *What if the smell taints other jackets? What if there were microbes on it and they infected other clothes?* It was a kind of hell that consumed his mind and soul every minute of every day.

It was so exhausting; one night, William just burst into tears. That's when he realized he needed help. It was the second time he had seen a psychiatrist. He was only nine the first time; he'd started bawling his eyes out at an exam, terrified of his father, who had hit the roof after William got a B from the previous one.

"If you're not first, you're last! There's no second

place in life; only winners and losers! Me, always top of my class, and my son gets a B! What a disappointment…"

His teacher's efforts to calm him down had been futile, and contacting his father to come and get him had only made things worse. The boy was taken to his father's friend Doctor Meinheimer. William still remembered waiting outside anxiously as his father talked to the psychiatrist. He never knew what had been said except that nothing had changed afterwards.

On the second occasion, the psychiatrist had listened for ten minutes at most, just the symptoms of his illness and had sent him away with a prescription of two different types of medication, one of which listed *suicide* as a side-effect. William had used them for a few months and stopped when he felt better. It had only kept the disease at bay for a year and the whole cycle had started again and again and again. Shrink after shrink, drugs on top of drugs. It went on like this for more than ten years.

The miracle cure had come after Charlie was born. One day, the six-month-old had dribbled on William's most treasured work suit. What could have been the end of a perfectly good jacket had failed to annoy him at all. Paternal love had beaten the disease, something he never would have expected to overcome – those vicious little rats gnawing at his mind. How had he been unable to see it before? That was when he realized it was possible to love someone more than himself.

It was only then he had started to analyze why he was so obsessed with being perfect. Perfectly clean, perfectly arranged, perfectly ordered, and perfectly neat. He had had to be perfect in every way to be accepted, admired and loved. He had needed other people's acceptance.

But why? What had made him feel so inadequate that he had needed to close the gap with external perfection?

"How dare you get a B in math, huh? Do you want to grow up to be a dumb-ass?"

"Button up your jacket! Straighten your tie!"

"What would people think if you wore this?"

"This music is too low class for our family!"

"How can you laugh at this garbage?"

"Sit up! Stand straight! Eat neatly! Behave yourself!"

Bawled out, belittled, humiliated, persecuted: it had all resounded in his mind at once. The traumas no children should have to suffer. That was it. That was what had destroyed his self-respect and confidence, left a void he had wanted to fill with the mask of elegance.

It was that young creature with tiny hands that finally helped him feel complete, adequate. That infant didn't care about the length of his trousers or the flawlessness of his skin; all he cared about was his love. There was no judgement; his son loved him just as he was, not as someone he wanted to be.

The obsession had gone away, but not the depression.

He got out of the shower and dried himself. He looked at his reflection in the mirror and saw the wrinkles on his forehead, the bags under his eyes. When had he grown old? Where did the shine in his eyes go? *All I want is to crawl back into bed and sleep till night.*

Rachel's voice interrupted his thoughts.

"Breakfast is ready; hurry up."

Hurry up? ... Why? To rush into another day in the cage?

He considered his options briefly. What if he called in sick? But the chains of life were dragging him. Like a galley slave who had to carry on and on and on.

"Coming!" William yelled back.

What if I suddenly had an awful headache? No; Rachel would insist I saw the doctor then. Fuck!

He got dressed, combed his thinning hair and ran downstairs.

Breakfasts were pretty standard on weekdays. Basic stuff, nothing yummy, so that he could have the right to have pancakes on weekends. They all ate quickly, said their goodbyes and left.

William always kissed his family before leaving; he'd always turn around at the door and mouth a silent *I love you*. He did it every time he parted from them, even for a day: it could be the last time he'd ever see them. He wanted to remember their image as the last thing he would ever think of in case he were to meet his death that day.

He got in his car and drove out of the garage. The routine had kicked in again.

Little did he know that this was to be the last ordinary day of his life.

He was stuck in traffic. He didn't mind; the longer it took him to get there, the better.

He was listening to *A Change of Seasons* by Dream Theater. The godfathers of progressive metal. Each member was a musical genius and virtuoso in his own right. To be honest, William was an unlikely metalhead, with all his wealth and sartorial elegance; yet he was precisely that, and had been since childhood. Even his wife had joined in the universal consternation and the label of *disturbed* caused by that taste in music. His father had once called him satanist. But William didn't care.

How could anyone not be disturbed by the state of the world, he thought.

In his view, heavy metal was the most sophisticated and profound genre of all. The lyrics, the composition, everything was rich with meaning. It resounded far more powerfully than the saccharine of pop trash: four verses of *oohs*, *yeahs*, and *shake dat ass babys* in endless repetitions of four chords...

Heavy metal, on the other hand, was concerned with the world's problems, inner emotions and all aspects of life. Its complexity and vast range of sentiments mirrored the world in all its nakedness. It was the reflection of society, politics, culture, science, history, and everything in between. The heavy bit was the after effect of living with disappointments, wasted years, harshness, and bitterness. For William, heavy metal was the music of everything. And that particular song was the epitome of metal.

I remember a time
My frail, virgin mind
Watched the crimson sunrise
Imagined what it might find
Life was filled with wonder
I felt the warm wind blow
I must explore the boundaries
Transcend the depth of winter's snow
In my den of inequity
Viciousness and subtlety
Struggle to ease the pain
Struggle to find the same
Ignorance surrounding me
I've never been so filled with fear
All my life's been drained from me
The end is drawing near...

The words of a poet, he thought, singing along.

His memory was the type that responded to music; he may struggle to remember what he had for lunch the other day, but once he heard a tune, he would be transported to that exact moment. A special one, in this case.

Innocence caressing me
I never felt so young before
There was so much life in me
Still I longed to search for more

The first time he had heard it, he was in love. At a time when he fell in love every other month. All head over heels, all of them fleeting, yet love all the same. He remembered plucking up the courage to call the blonde beauty he fell for, only to get her mother on the phone; the girl was out, her mother would tell her that he'd called. William hovered by the telephone for two nights in a row, playing that song repeatedly. She rang back on the third. He got the girl, but none of the moments of that brief romance could match those three magical nights. Not even close. It was not the girl the song reminded him of now, but the sublime melancholy of a fifteen-year-old, desperate to make a move, a song playing repeatedly on the stereo, and falling asleep dog tired.

How he missed those innocent days filled with hope and joy. How he longed to be that boy again and feel the pureness. No worries for the future, no responsibilities other than some irrelevant exams, only the thrill of love, that tingling in his chest and the sweet sensation of freedom.

But those days are gone now
Changed like a leaf on a tree
Blown away forever
Into the cool autumn breeze
The snow has now fallen
And my sun's not so bright
I struggle to hold on
With the last of my might

Verses that always filled the gloomy liquid in his eyes. Every single time.

He was lost in the music, his eyes glazed over, when he caught sight of a kid on the bus next to his car. A boy who looked no more than seventeen and was wearing headphones. A boy with a discomforting stare, William thought. It had happened on more than one occasion and he had felt the same every time. He remembered what he was like at the same age. Driving his sports car to school, with girls beside him, partying every night without a worry in the world.

This boy, however, did not look like he was enjoying his youth. He looked exhausted and weary. His eyes did not shine as they should have at that age. *How could this be fair?* he thought.

"The world isn't fair!" he heard his father's voice.

And why not? He realized maybe he didn't know the real world as it was, not even at this age. Was this a blessing or a curse? He did not know.

"Men should be strong! Only the strong survive. You'll end up a loser if you're not."

"Shut up!" William warned the voice in his head.

"A man can't be sentimental. He'd be trodden on if he was. Life has no time for losers; it chews them up and spits them out. Stop acting like a sissy and man up!"

"Shut the fuck up! You're dead!" screamed William silently.

"Come on, man, move!" yelled the guy in the car behind him, blowing his horn like mad. Realizing the traffic jam had cleared, William pulled himself together and resumed driving.

It took another fifteen minutes to reach work. His company owned the building but only occupied five floors; the remaining twenty-five were let out. It was his father's first big project after deciding to move from suburban house construction to big city skyscrapers thirty years ago. That's where the real money was, after all. This building had brought his father great success and fame, transforming him from small-time contractor to property mogul in just five years as more of his tremendous buildings rose all over the city. How he financed all these projects, starting with the first one, had always remained a controversial topic among the city's society. Rumors ranged from mafia involvement to defrauding the banks to money laundering… No one, not even William, knew the truth. He had never had the courage to ask his father. They never had the warm relationship William had with his own children. His father was very strict, with a quick temper and a cold personality. The kind of guy who viewed tenderness – even to his own child – as a weakness. The kind of guy who petted his son only in sleep, not that William remembered such an occasion. His father was in love with himself and expected total obeisance from everyone just because he was successful. If you didn't, you'd find yourself locked in the bathroom for hours. A cruel, mean guy.

These days, no one cared about the allegations any longer; they were rich and powerful, and that was all that mattered. But William always felt sick to his stomach watching the company video in the elevator every morning on his way up. The video that presented his father as a saint, one of the great men of his time who had founded an empire. Every time he saw that video, his heart sank with an inexplicable type of shame. Something didn't smell right in that script. At the very least, the smiling *great man* in that video was not the same man he knew as father.

"Good morning, sir. How are you today?" greeted the doorman. William loathed that outfit modeled like a palace guard uniform.

"Good morning, Eduardo, I'm good, thanks. And you?" he replied. It was essential to treat his staff with courtesy, especially if they were on the lower levels of the food chain. Wealth came with its responsibilities. And he always smiled back, even if it was just another mandatory mask.

He changed his mind about asking the doorman about his wife and children; he couldn't remember if it was this one who had kids or the guy on the night shift.

"Have a nice day, sir," said Eduardo, opening the door.

With a "Thank you, Eduardo, you too," William headed towards the elevator. The goddamn elevator with that goddamn fake video.

Why not nix it? he thought, *I'm the boss now!*

"What would people say?!" he heard his mother's voice. His mother who was always in league with the cruel man. The mother whose silence denied him the protection he needed.

"Appearances are everything, son! Don't you forget it now! Enemies are everywhere and they want what we have; we always need to look our strongest, our best! The slightest hint of weakness and they'll swarm us like cockroaches to sugar. And don't you dare challenge me again; I was building this business while you were motorboating cheerleaders' tits!"

His head rang with his father's roar, furious with William for daring to disagree with him on a business matter in front of others.

I can't, thought William, *Anyone can see why I did. He's thought of as this great big man, disappointed in his spoiled no good of a son, who is mediocre at best. It's no contest; even with him dead, I still lose.*

All the way up thirty floors, he avoided looking at that small screen. The door opened straight onto his floor. He walked in reluctantly, the foolishly cheerful voice of the woman on the video in his ears until the door closed again.

In the Rudned Development Group, we always value people over money; a legacy passed down to us from our founder, the legendary Daniel Rudned.

"Yeah, right," murmured William.

"What's that, Mr. Rudned?" his secretary asked.

"Nothing Janine, good morning," said William.

"Sorry sir, good morning to you too," Janine replied.

"May I have some coffee, please?"

"Of course, sir, right away," Janine said.

Janine was relatively new. Following his father's untimely – and sudden – death over a year ago, William had moved into the old man's office and kept his father's secretary Rose for a while. A grumpy old woman with a constant frown. But it didn't work out. Rose was nearly sixty; she had known William since he was in shorts. It was awkward for both of them. Moreover, it was she who, since he was a youth, had sent all those withering emails from his father. The old man didn't even have the courtesy to write his own.

Every single mischief of his, therefore, was known to Rose. Bad for chain of command. All the same, he had to give it at least six months. It wouldn't be appropriate to let go of her sooner. *What would people say?*

The twenty-five-year old Janine, on the other hand, was a much brighter personality. It was much easier to issue her instructions, and she knew nothing about him either.

He entered his office and turned on the TV. He always kept it on all day in mute, so he'd know straightaway if anything important happened during the day. Yeah, right: like they told the truth! At least it was more entertaining than Twitter.

"With tensions rising between Russia and Ukraine, financial markets are in turmoil as stock exchanges struggle to find a direction," said the newsreader.

"Good morning, big boss," said Mark, stepping in.

Mark was one of William's oldest friends and colleagues. Much valued as his father's right-hand man for nearly twenty years. Rising above an impoverished background, Mark excelled at school, thanks in part to a scholarship from Daniel Rudned, started to work for his benefactor immediately after his graduation, soon proved himself to be the golden child and worked his way up.

With complete trust in Mark, Daniel had placed William under his tutelage when he joined his father's business. William was thirty by then; after several unsuccessful starts on his own, he'd had to crawl back to the security of his family business when Charlie was born.

"It's so much different from the old days, William. Competition is fierce. They're really hungry out there. Guys with nothing to lose and everything to gain. I'm sorry; but I will not finance you. Your business plan sucks. · You don't have the makings of an entrepreneur; sad but true."

These were his father's exact words when William had explained his business plan and asked for a loan. Daniel had refused, William had countered with the offer of a partnership, and Daniel had just laughed. That's when William made a vow to work hard, be successful, earn his freedom and shove that fucking grin back into his father's mouth.

Failure to achieve that goal nearly destroyed him. Destroyed his self-confidence and self-respect, at the very least. Going to his father with his tail between his legs was the hardest and most humiliating thing he'd done. It also triggered the peak of his chronic depression.

That deep wound never healed completely. The biggest embarrassment of his life. He had fought for his independence in the world and failed.

What a loser son to a great man.

When he started at his family firm, he was anxious and a little offended at becoming sidekick to a man only a few years older. Thankfully Mark turned out to be a great guy and a good friend. Without ever looking down on him, Mark taught him everything he needed to know. He was happy when William came on top. But deep down, William always knew that if Mark had been blood, he would have inherited the captain's chair.

"Morning Mark," said William, "Coffee? I just asked for some."

"Sure, make it black, though; it was a long night!" said Mark.

A bachelor and a ladies' man, Mark partied hard and loved his liquor. Even so, William never saw him be late for work, hungover or underperform. *It must be his genes*, he thought. As for him, he could no longer handle two whiskeys; he always needed his seven hours of sleep, yet here was a guy five years his senior getting it done until morning and showing up at work full capacity like it was nothing.

"Blonde or brunette?" he asked, chuckling.

"Neither! She was a redhead!" answered Mark, "They are the hottest! Got this fire inside that never goes out. They are the ultimate lovemaking machines, I'm telling you. Freckles on her ass and everything!"

They both guffawed like a couple of idiots. Boys will be boys.

"I envy you, man; last time I did anything like that was fifteen years ago," said William.

"Don't; I mean it. Sure, it sounds fun and all but after a while, it gets dull. I yearn to lie beside a girl just to smell her hair," said Mark.

"Says the guy who gets laid every single night!" William smiled, "What's with you bachelors and your desire for a decent girl. If you want one, go ahead and find her already and stop whining."

"It's not that easy. The girls today, oh, they are little devils. Hard to tell the good ones apart. Hard to tell if they really love you or are just gold diggers. And anyway, at my age, I don't know if I can cope with having kids. And believe me, the first thing at the back of their minds are kids," said Mark.

Finally, something William had that Mark didn't. And he was right. It was hard to read people's intentions these days. Everyone was obsessed with the good life. Romanticism in this age was a fool's dream. William considered himself fortunate to have a family. He knew he was lucky to have Rachel. She was an incredible wife and mother. She was the most selfless and considerate human being William knew. And he knew that she loved her for who he was, not for what he had. He had known it from the moment he proposed. Rachel had said yes without blinking. He always remembered that moment when he was angry or cross with her. Even if she had all the peculiarities of a typical woman, Rachel always put William and her family first. She supported him during his struggle to start his own business. She always stood by him, no matter what. She even left her law practice when Charlie was born, determined to tend to their son's every need; she refused to have nannies, even when they had the means. But over the years, as William sank deeper into depression, he had grown more and more distant. As if he was detaching himself from the world. His melancholy and sadness affected their marriage.

Rachel knew everything about him. His dreadful childhood, his disturbed psyche, his frustration with life, his lack of self-confidence and the darkness dormant inside. But knowing and understanding were two different animals. Some things can only be lived, otherwise can't be known. It was not her fault. She had a loving family and a wonderful childhood. She never needed to seek meaning in, or the reason for, her existence. Being alive, healthy and with loved ones was more than enough for her. It was not that she couldn't carry him; she just couldn't handle him. She was a creature of the external world, whereas William was a creature lost in the abyss of its unknowns.

"You may be right," said William.

"You know the saying: a man is incomplete until he's married. Afterwards, he's finished," said Mark. They laughed again.

"Look at this shit!" said William, pointing out to the TV, "Here we are, on the brink of World War Three, and they're still on about where stocks will be tomorrow. What good will money do if we're all destroyed? It's bullshit."

"Well, another quote then: When all else fails, there's always delusion, right?"

"Exactly! It's all a delusion, after all. I wonder more and more about what the world has become, Mark. The more I think, the gloomier I get."

"Don't be so hard on yourself, William; it's not your responsibility to save the world," Mark replied.

"Whose then, those crooked politicians? All they care about are the chairs they sit on. I'm telling you; things can't go on like this. Look at the headlines. All kinds of horrors around the world. Poverty, crimes against humanity, war crimes, drought, social injustice, rape, murders, genocides in the name of God, for Christ's sake. They kill babies somewhere right this moment. Everyone's out there for their own. Empathy's gone. It's like we're going backward in time to the dark ages in our spiritual world. Nothing matters but money now," said William.

"Wow, easy, tiger. What's got into you? What's with all this heavy stuff? Come on, calm down, chill," said a worried Mark.

"That's just it: I can't. I can't just sit back and live in peace while everything goes to shit," replied William in despair.

"Let me take you out tonight; you look in need of blowing off steam."

"I can't. It's spaghetti night," smiled William.

"Well, at least have a glass of wine with it, OK? You look really stressed. We need you clear headed; we got lots to do in the coming weeks, remember?"

Mark was right; they had a big deal going on. A deal his father had started. The biggest and most complex construction project they had ever undertaken. Once finished, it would be the most luxurious residence in the country. Except, it gave William no excitement. It was his father's dream, not his. Charging rich assholes eight million dollars for 4,000 square feet of living space seemed like fraud. Each apartment cost little more than one million. The rest was for the name and location. People lost their homes every day, families were destroyed; and here they were, ripping off people for an amount that could change the lives of a hundred families.

What a world.

"Don't worry, got my eye on the ball," William assured him.

"They better be; we've invested a shedload in this one," Mark replied, "All right, I leave you to your thoughts then; remember, meeting with the bank tomorrow morning. I have the presentation ready; I'll share it with you today."

"Thanks, Mark, I mean it," said William gratefully.

"No problem. And if you change your mind about tonight, let me know beforehand, OK? I need to cancel a certain brunette if you do," Mark said with a mischievous smile.

"Yeah, yeah; now get out of here!" William smiled back.

As Mark headed to the door, William took out his smartphone to open the news app.

Smartphone. What an ironic name for a device that makes people stupider than ever. He took care to avoid being addicted to that self-slavery chain. He likened anyone with heads locked onto their screens to cyborgs. In all honesty, weren't people part cyborgs now? They walked with a device in their hands. A device they slept with, socialized with, lived with every minute of their lives, recording every moment of their lives on without truly living in those moments, getting lost in that rabbit hole well beyond the imagination of Lewis Carroll. People were now totally dependent on a machine. Who needed dystopic science fiction movies when machines had already taken over their lives? It was all here already.

He knew he was also hooked on it to a degree. He had a ritual. A ritual he had to fulfill every day, all day long. Starting with the events of the world, going onto the hate and concluding with the daily circus show of the flesh freaks.

Browsing the news, his first stop, proved to be increasingly distressful.

Ex-Marine sentenced to 210 years for raping and beating Cambodian children

Estimated one million Afghan children in slave labor

Myanmar military committed war crimes in Karenni state

Russia Accelerates Troop Buildup Along Ukraine Border

Texas Sues Meta Over Facebook's Facial-Recognition Practices

Israeli missiles strike Syrian town south of Damascus

WHO says global case decline affected by drop in testing, deaths still alarmingly high

Driest season for over 22 years

Employees fire over wage increase demand arrested for protesting at headquarters

Connecticut socialite mom admits to secretly filming minors in her mansion

China changed the ending of Fight Club. No building explosions.

"What the... ?" William exclaimed before carrying on.

China has changed the ending of the popular cult movie by cutting the last scene and telling viewers "Police rapidly figured out the whole plan and arrested all criminals."

"Ha-ha-ha, holy shit! Hilarious and terrifying at the same time," he said to himself. He couldn't help but laugh at an incredibly disturbing censor of an oppressive government. *Fight Club* was one of his favorite movies of all time; imagining hearing those ridiculous words as the ending of a masterpiece just made it more ludicrous than bothersome. *What a world.*

The smile caused by this last item was soon wiped away by the others. He closed down the app at once. Opened Twitter instead. This was the second part of the ritual. *What were his fellow men thinking today*, he wondered, hurrying to scan the tags. He wanted to get on with it as soon as possible.

#War
#Nuclear
#FedUpWithYou
#YouWillPay
#Trump4Life
#Kanye
#CardiB
#ArrestHillary

#Cleavage
#KnowYourPlace

His kin didn't disappoint. They were still as hateful, ignorant and careless as ever.

The last stop of the ritual was Instagram, images of happy people to lighten his mood. He knew they were fake but it helped him forget the nasty stuff, even for a short while. Everyone wanted to show how beautiful, talented and special they were, thanking God, celebrating life... Wannabe gurus, paragons of wisdom, narcissist flesh dealers. Mass-produced stereotypes that feed on digital thumbs. He felt sick but the ritual was complete.

Now it was time to get back to work. He tried to read the daily reports of sales, costs, profits, and ongoing projects. This was his duty as chairman. And he did his job. But he despised every minute of it. Then he opened the news app again. He couldn't stop himself from going back to something that made him miserable over and over again. Clear definition of a compulsion to satisfy an obsession. Then Twitter, then Instagram, then reports again. Ritual after ritual, all day long. Hell took shape as repetition. And that scream in the background of his mind:

What is the point of it all? How does my work contribute to the world? How usefully do I spend my time and energy? How can I sit here, idly, motivated solely by profit while people are devoured by the world? God, I hate it, I hate being here, I hate this job. I don't belong here.

A day like any other. Repetition like a timepiece ticking with no more intention than to move in a never-ending circle. Nothing was gained at the end and nothing was lost.

At long last, his periodic observation of a twenty-something thousand dollar Swiss watch came to an end. It was 6 o'clock. Spaghetti night started around 7.30. He still had time. It was winter and already dark, although it was a mild evening. So he headed for a bench by the lake in front of his office to smoke a cigar. One of the highlights of his day. All alone and left with his thoughts. He could smoke a cigar in an hour and easily be home by 7.30. He took out the cigar from its case and leant back on the bench. He punched the tip, pulled his gold flame torch out of the three-thousand-dollar cashmere coat and started to light that forty-dollar cigar. It took more than a minute; it was important to light it evenly around the tip. This ceremony was an important part of the process to enjoy the smooth leaves that had been grown for at least five seasons in a far distant land called Cuba and harvested before spending another two seasons in fermentation, and were finally rolled in the skillful hands of a master who could never afford one single such stick with a month's wage.

William was ready for some me time.

At first, he didn't notice the lady approaching him and sitting on the other end of the bench. Not until she crossed her legs. He had yet to look at her, but the movement caught his eye.

Why the hell would you sit on this bench when there are plenty more nearby? he thought; it was rude. He wanted to be left alone. Now he had to nod politely at the very least to show he was OK with her sitting next to him.

Those uncomfortable thoughts vanished the moment he moved his head to look at her. The planned nod did not come.

William had seen his fill of beautiful women, but never someone like her. Her fiery long red hair, stature and face were mesmerizing. Her big eyes, pink skin, cherry lips, and small nose were harmonious enough to be the dream of any obsessive-compulsive. Her height, statuesque figure and legs looked unreal. She looked like a warrior princess who had jumped out of a manga. She was pure beauty and a vamp at the same time. She looked delicate as a flower yet powerful as a lioness.

William realized that not only he had failed to nod but was also frozen, gaping at her. He was in a kind of deep trance. Not as in love at first sight, more like the way time freezes when you look at a masterpiece.

He was virtually hypnotized enough to find nothing out of the ordinary in those flint-hard eyes. Yet they were unnaturally yellow. A bright, bitter reptilian yellow.

Only when she started talking did he pull himself together.

"Hello," she said.

"Hi...," said William. This time his gaze fell on her outfit. An elegant, business-like two-piece in a dark red. Probably another white collar slave just released from her torture chamber, although the suit looked a little unusual for work. It was a bit fancy. And her legs... Her glossy, tapering, long legs.

"Rough day?" she asked him.

"As rough as the last and the next," said William with a shy smile.

"I hear you. Well, my own's about to start soon; I'm sure it'll be hard as nails for me too," she said. It sounded bizarre. Who would start their day after seven? Only night shift nurses, hostesses in fancy restaurants or hookers. And this extraordinary specimen was no nurse. Which meant she was either a hostess or...

Holy shit, is she... ?

Her decisive voice interrupted his thoughts, "So what do you do?"

Goddammit! Another small talk pretending to care and love what I have to put up with all day. And probably all for a whore who'll split the moment she knows I'm not interested.

His upbringing would never let him patronize anyone, though, not even a prostitute.

"I'm in development," he replied.

"Wow, exciting! What kind of development?"

William's suspicions weren't that baseless after all. She wanted to know if he could afford her for the night.

"Well, we mainly build skyscrapers. On occasion, we also build wide complexes like malls," he replied. The killer punch had to be coming now. She must have smelled the money and was about to make the move: flatter him to raise her rate. He was almost sure of it.

As his thoughts took shape, William looked at her feet. He had always had a thing for them, even to the point of fetishism; he enjoyed taking a guess at people's ancestry from the shape of their feet. If the second toe was longer than the big toe, it was called a Greek foot; if the first three were all the same length, Roman; and if the toes tapered from the big toe to the little toe, Egyptian. He could list at least seven ancestries from foot shapes. But this one… this one was different. He scanned his brain for all he knew about feet; to no avail. It was a first. Her feet were slender, all the toes were nearly the same length, yet nothing looked out of place or deformed in any way. They were long but not stocky. All in all, they were beautiful. *Bizarrely erotic*, he thought.

"Great; and do you love it?" she asked.

This question threw him off balance. No one, not even his own wife ever really asked if he loved what he did. But now, this classy hooker whom he'd just met was asking if he loved his work. Not what his position was, or if he was making good money; but if he loved it.

"Sure. Building something is very satisfying, even if it really is a pain in the ass," William said with a Pan Am smile.

It made her laugh out loud. William, who usually avoided slang in talking to strangers, surprised himself with this sense of ease in her company. He replied with a loud laugh of his own, although he knew the only truthful part in his reply was *the pain in the ass* bit.

"Your eyes say otherwise, though," she said more somberly this time.

"What do you mean?" asked William with a nervous half smile.

"You don't have the looks of someone who loves how his days go."

"How can you know something like this?" asked William, the earlier ease blowing away piece by piece.

"Call it intuition," she replied.

"Well, there are good days and hard days, as with everyone's job. What do you do?" asked William without thinking and regretted it right away. *What if she was… ?*

"I'm what you call a life coach," she answered before he could complete his thought. It was a bit of a relief, but still hard to figure out what a life coach would be doing at this hour.

"Interesting. I do know a few life coaches," he bragged, having met some at fundraisers. No matter how little he thought of those charlatans, name-dropping did serve to conceal his own insecurities.

"And what do you think about them?" she asked straightaway.

William paused, feeling himself going pale.

"Don't worry, I'm accustomed to derision; feel free to give me your honest opinion."

"Well, I respect what you're doing but most life coaches I met were full of shit; no offense," he replied.

She laughed loudly again. It relaxed him; he had not offended her. Confrontation was not his strong suit.

"None taken; most of the so-called life coaches only

repeat what they read in *Cosmo* to their clients, just in a fancier way. I, on the other hand, take a different approach."

"Yeah? What kind of approach?" asked William. For some reason, he was enjoying an intriguing conversation with a woman whose name he didn't even know.

"I only coach the most promising people. I choose my own clients well before they know they need me. And I always coach through an immersive experience, not with sweet platitudes."

"Uh, well, this is a first. I guess that's why you said your day was just starting? I mean, you have a client for tonight, right?"

"Yes, I do, William. This one's going to be very special. A once-in-a-lifetime occasion."

"Great, I hope it goes well," he replied, before realizing something was wrong. His face twisted in confusion:

"Sorry, but… how do you know my name?" he asked, trying to hide his perplexity.

"Oh, I know a great deal about you, William. I've been looking forward to this moment for a long time," said the beautiful woman.

"What do you mean? I don't understand," he asked. He was still trying to be polite with a fake smile on his face. But the confusion in his voice was getting a little harder to hide.

"You will. When it's all over. For now, all you need to know is I'm here only for you."

"I have no idea what you are talking about, seriously," he said with a nervous smile this time, still hanging on to the pretense of courtesy.

"You are my client for tonight, William. We'll go on a grand journey together."

"Ha-ha-ha, very funny. Who put you up to this? Was it Mark?" asked William with an uncomfortable sneer. The polite smile now looked pathetically confused and vexed.

"No, William, this was always meant to be. Designed from the moment you were born. This is the moment you start fulfilling your destiny, your purpose," was the calm reply, "I'm here to put back into you the spark you'd lost, and stoke it until it turns into a raging fire which consumes everything in its path and erases the mist covering your sight so that you can do the same to others."

"Madam, I've enjoyed your company so far, but this is getting to be a little uncomfortable now. Who the hell are you?"

"My name is Milena, William, and believe you me, this is no joke. I'm not here to comfort you. I'm not your friend. I am everything people around you are not. I'm honest, harsh, unbiased, and unafraid. I do not care of the consequences of my actions," said the crimson goddess, looking a little intimidating.

"Look, Milena – or whoever the hell you are, I will be saying this in the politest way I can think of. Please stop this stupid shit and leave me alone," William replied. Now the smile was all but gone, leaving him looking a good deal more serious.

"I'm afraid I can't do that, William. We have a lot of work to do, you and I."

William gave a tense titter. Curious as he was about what was going on, he'd had enough of it – whatever it was. He was clearly being played by this nutter or worse: any second now, he'd be abducted or robbed by some guys using this gorgeous woman as a distraction. Maybe the plan was to put William into bed with her, shoot their playtime photos and blackmail him. All kinds of nasty scenarios were rushing into his mind, sharp as stomach cramps. It was starting to get scary. In any case, he didn't need this right now; it was time to call it quits and go home and quick. At least he'd have something to tell Mark the next day.

"OK. Well, it was nice knowing you. And thanks for ruining my cigar pleasure. I'll be leaving now," said William without looking at her face. It was uncomfortable before but now it was annoying, even a little scary.

He got up, turned back to scan his surroundings for thugs lurking in the shadows, and saw none. Just as he had set off for the road in brisk steps, he felt a hand on his left shoulder. A blinding light flashed in his eyes. His body felt as though it was torn into its atoms. Like every molecule in his body was vibrating at the same time. He felt no pain but for a brief second, he felt empty. Like he was non-existent in a universe full of matter.

The next thing he saw was the vast emptiness of dust around him. His eyes were seeing but his mind couldn't comprehend what had happened or where he was.

He was in the middle of a desert.

He had always found peace in empty spaces. And deserts were his favorite. He had once stared at the Sahara from an airplane. Watched the emptiness for miles from his porthole and found it pure beauty and simplicity. No chaos, no ringing telephones, no car horns, no people. It was total serenity.

But now, there was a bitter taste in his mouth. His pulse was fast enough to make him think he was about to crash. He had felt like this once before, on a treadmill, running fast to burn more calories. It was June and he'd had to be ripped for the beach, with a six-pack. He still had a lot of fat around the waist, which was why he was running like mad. That run had turned into a challenge. It was then that he had felt like his heart was about to burst. He had tasted acid in his mouth. Now that acid was back and his mind was like a frozen old computer screen, where the only way to fix it was to restart the system.

"Well, I hope this is proof enough for you. Now

shall we begin?" said the angelic voice issuing from the extraordinarily symmetrical lips.

William gaped at the woman, who was now sitting still on a dusty hill. She was no longer in the suit but something like an armor which bared her belly, arms and legs. Her sandals displayed those feet in their splendor. This was the first supernatural thing that had happened to William in his forty-two years in this world, and he couldn't take his eyes off her. She was utterly, incredibly and magically beautiful. The skin covering her muscular body looked like velvet. For a split second, all he could think of was kissing her on the sands for hours on end. But reality beckoned; his eyes stung with the sand blowing around. Then he exclaimed like a madman, his head spinning in every direction.

"What the fuck is happening?! Where am I? What happened?! Oh my God!"

Hearing his own voice, he was reminded of an episode of *The Sopranos*, where a foolish young thug steps on the wrong foot and is about to be shot by the main character Tony Soprano – or as they said, *about to get whacked*. The moment the wannabe gangster realizes he was being killed, he hollers "Mommy!" That scene had given William the most unpleasant chill. It had made him think of his own son, Charlie, who was only three months old at the time. What if his boy had been in a situation like that? What if he had been killed like that young thug? He was constantly scared of losing his beloved son. He had watched that scene on the verge of tears.

Now he felt like that young thug. He was terrified. The only names he wanted to plead for, however, before his imminent death were his children's.

"You were about to leave. I had to convince you that this is real. So I took you to a place you found peaceful. Now get yourself together. We need to start."

"Start what?" He still sounded between despair and fear.

"Our task ahead, of course, you silly boy."

"What task?" asked William without thinking. His shaky tone had a hint of a something calmer now. Calmer as much as it could be in a surreal situation like that. But the fear was still there and Milena could smell it.

"The debate you've had all your life. All the whys, all the whats, all the hows… But this time, you will have me to debate with, not just your pathetic self. And I'll ride you like a bull till we reach our destination," she said. Her yellow eyes now looked sharper.

"What is our destination? What is happening? Please tell me. Or better yet, take me back. Oh, yeah, take me back now; I want to wake up. Oh, yes, sir, I want to wake up right now!" he said with a shudder. His face was white as snow. Like all his blood had drained. For a moment, he wondered if he had been drugged and was hallucinating.

"I will explain everything. But first things first. We are not going anywhere, William, and you're not asleep. So stop your whining," she said angrily, "In order to understand what's happening, though, you need to keep an open mind. Can you do that, William?"

"I honestly don't know. I don't feel like my mind is in any state to evaluate anything at the moment," said William. His eyes were filling up not because he was about to cry, but because he felt like a newborn baby, not knowing where he is or what's happening after leaving a cramped but protective environment which had defined his life for nine months.

"As I said before, my name is Milena, William. I am what you might call a demon. I will assist you to create the manifesto of the new world order. You were born to transform this wretched, stinking world into an oasis. And I was created to help you achieve that," said the velvet-skinned creature, "You and I will change the world, William. We will stop suffering and pain. We will usher in a new era for humankind. An era full of meaning, purpose and freedom. We will save them all, William," she said with a confident smile on her cherry lips, "My sole purpose of existence is to crack you open with whatever means necessary. I don't care if you suffer in the process. My only concern is to get you out of your shell. And I will not stop until I do. So, shall we begin?"

William could not stop a smile. It held no joy though. Rather, it was a wry smile, an effort to hide the sickly fear behind it. He briefly considered running like hell. *But where?* Wherever he looked, all he could see was an endless desert. His inner voice came to the rescue, channeling the primeval instinct (fight or flight?) into a more rational method. A method to use reason to justify denying the situation. Reason was the foundation of civilized men to overcome obstacles in life, after all. And this, as irrational as it seemed, was just an obstacle, nothing more.

"Wait a minute!" said William, gathering more confidence than he had so far since the start of this nightmare, "I'm forty-two years old. I don't amount to anything other than maybe a good father. I'm not even a good husband. I didn't achieve anything extraordinary in my life. I'm not sure how I could make a living if I wasn't born wealthy. I'm no one special. I'm as ordinary as they come. And a coward besides. I have always been scared of everything. Confrontation, standing up for my right, speaking up; everything! How the hell am I going to change the world? This is bullshit." This time, all he could think of was how absurd all this was. So it must have been a dream. Yes, it certainly was. He was ready to wake up now.

"With my guidance and help, William," said the woman who called herself Milena.

"But you say you're a demon. Demons are supposed to be evil. Always mischievous with a secret agenda. Demons manipulate. And demons certainly don't help people or work for the betterment of humankind. Why would a demon do anything you claim to do for me?" He was still trying to rationalize his way out of this horribly idiotic dream. He'd had extremely vivid dreams before. This had to be just another one – an idea that calmed him down a bit.

"Because, Pups, there is a secret tune in the center of the universe and it sounds like perfect balance. Everything in the cosmos has two sides. Without darkness, there would be no light. Without evil, there would be no good. And what is evil or good? Who decides if something is good or evil? These are merely names people invented for order and control. There is no evil; there is no good, there is only power," said Milena. She now sounded far wiser than suggested by the slutty looks.

"No, there is a distinct difference between good and evil. You can't have a perspective for some of the evil. Killing is evil. There is no way around it," replied William, feeling like he was warming up to this game.

"Oh yeah? What about all the wars throughout millennia that killed millions? Were they all for the sake of evil?" snapped Milena. The quickness of the reply did no good to William's already fragile confidence.

"No, most of them were for freedom, for independence from tranny. People fought two world wars to protect freedom and democracy," said William, with the real answer hanging behind his mind. He knew it was not so, as did she. He was a little embarrassed to lie for the sake of winning. Such a poor lie too, with no solid backing.

"What about the ones before? What about the holy crusades? Were they also undertaken to protect democracy?" asked Milena, just as he'd predicted she would.

"No, of course not; they were arrogant and ignorant people of the time, believing killing was justified so long as it was done in the name of God," he replied. He knew it wasn't going to hold water.

"So they were evil then? Does ignorance justify impaling newborn babies and crucifying people just because they believed in another god?" asked Milena. William was beginning to find her rapid answers increasingly intolerable.

"No, of course not. Those people were evil. Even ignorance has its limits. Someone impaling babies has no empathy whatsoever, therefore, evil," William replied again. But he knew he had messed up.

"So; if killing in the name of religion is evil, doesn't that make religion itself evil?" asked the demon. William could smell his defeat in her smile.

"No, that's not what I meant and you know it. You're twisting my words. All I'm saying is killing is evil. No matter the reason," he replied in a last attempt to save face, even though he knew he had sacrificed logic in favor of a quick reply. He was sinking deeper as he struggled to continue. It would be great to change the subject now.

"But killing for freedom is not? You said it yourself. Is killing justified when it's for freedom and against tranny but not for religion?" Oh, how smug that smile was.

"Well, yes... Killing evil is not evil. Hitler was evil."

William sounded more ridiculous by the minute.

"And so, all Germans were evil? Even the civilians? Because the allies killed more than half a million German civilians in the war. Targeted them deliberately. So if only Hitler and his high command were evil, shouldn't it be just them that were killed? Why all those others? And if they were evil, wouldn't the Germans realize it and kill him?" asked Milena.

"It's not that simple. For the Germans, Hitler was a savior, the redeemer of the German people," replied William. Was the misdirection working? He hoped so.

"You see, it's all subjective. Good or evil depend on perspective. The Germans supported Hitler when he invaded Poland and killed thousands. He massacred Jews and gypsies, babies and old people. Did they see these acts as evil? Did the Germans object? No, they did not. They were happy to rise from the ashes and humiliation of World War One and to be recognized as a world power again. And they would have continued to support him if he hadn't lost. So does this make them evil too?" asked the beautiful self-claimed demon.

Her smile almost wrote "I rest my case" on her mouth.

"I don't know. It's a complex subject. I'm not sure anyone can reach an absolute conclusion on this," said William. He had conceded.

"This is what I'm trying to explain, Pups. Evil, good, it's all relative for you, justified to serve your purposes. What is evil is just for another's benefit. What is just for you is evil for another. There is no absolute right or wrong in your minds. Even a serial killer has a purpose. Not for the sake of evil. For him, there is always a justifiable cause, even if he knows what he does is wrong. Unfortunately, the only thing that matters is power and the ones who hold it can justify their cause without being blamed for evil. The intention behind it is the true nature of evil or good. Nature kills every hour without distinction. The universe kills every second. Why? What is the reason? If we are born and in existence, why do we all die? Is it for the sake of another birth and continuity of the cosmos? Are we all born to die and die to be born then?" asked Milena.

William was lost, confused, with no idea where this was going. He most certainly wasn't enjoying it. Just as he was grappling for some clever retort, Milena interrupted.

"I'm so happy, William," she said, looking pleased.

"What? Why?" *What did happiness have to do with all this nonsense?*

"Don't you see? We started our quest about ten minutes ago. We're now ten minutes closer to getting you in shape," she explained.

"What did you mean by saving the world?" asked William defiantly, "You can't just say it with no explanation. Tell me more. What's happening here? I need to know, otherwise I'll go crazy. Tell me everything! I need to know, and now!" he demanded, frustrated.

"Fair enough," said Milena, "But you need to sit down."

William realized he was still standing tensely. His legs were rigid and all his muscles were stretched so taut they could snap, especially the piece of meat in his head. He was afraid if he sat down, he would lost control over this terrible dream and never woke up again. But he did it anyway. Curiosity had proved to be too powerful to resist.

"We have been here for a very long time, William," Milena started to explain, "We have observed your progress for thousands of years. At times, we offered guidance. Not to interfere but influence. However, you have come to a crossroads in your progress. Paths you will choose from now on will affect your future. And from where we are standing, your future doesn't look bright at all. Our hope and patience for your self-reliance grew very thin over the last century. So we decided to influence once again. And I have been commissioned to help you to reach a level of consciousness to influence your fellow humans, because otherwise..." Milena stopped abruptly as if the next thing she'd say would be devastating.

"Who do you mean by *we*? And otherwise, what?" asked William.

"The *we* part is not important. As for the otherwise part... Well, if you don't change direction in the near future, you will be destroyed," said Milena. She showed no joy in this revelation.

"What do you mean destroyed?" asked William, "What will you do? Obliterate the whole world?"

"Not the world, William. Just you, humans," answered Milena.

"Why? What's the purpose? What will you do when you wipe us all out: observe the termites?" asked William arrogantly, in another attempt to cover the growing fear in his voice. His eyes betrayed him, though.

"We won't have to do it, William; you are more than capable of doing it all by yourselves. And who says you are the first or the last for that matter, that occupied this little rock?" Milena replied.

William's eyes were no longer capable of concealing the fear. His hands were shaking.

"You're lying. If there had been others before us, we'd have found their traces. We would have proof of their existence. You're lying. You truly are a demon. Trying to manipulate me, are you?" asked William furiously, wanting to hide his fear behind anger. It was no use.

"Why would I lie to you? And, who said I was a demon? I only said I am what you might call a demon. Call me whatever you want. I only said a demon, because your understanding of my actions upon you will only be named as evil by your dogmatic beliefs. It doesn't necessarily mean my end goal is evil, though," answered Milena, "As for the traces of those before you: they're all around you. You're just conditioned by *them* to disregard those clues as hoaxes or conspiracy theories. In any case, none of it matters; what matters is your time is limited and it's high time we start to mold you into the man you were meant to be."

"Who do you mean by *them*?" asked William. Of all the things Milena mentioned, this was the most critical. Who were *they*?

"Oh, don't get me started on *them*," grinned Milena, "*They* are the ones you should get rid of if you want to see the light at the end of the tunnel. Oh, yeah, you definitely should. So let's see: who the hell could they be, those mischievous overlords?"

CHAPTER 2
LEGIO

For as long as William had known himself, he had felt alone, even when surrounded by family, friends and crowds. He had felt helpless. He had resented having no control over his life. Whenever he had decided to take the reins, someone had always blocked his way. Be it his family, his wife, society or the fucking Pope himself; it was always the same. His dreams shattered, his will broken and his spirit crushed.

"You are the master of your life…" he had once read in a so-called guru's book. He had read it over and over again, as if repetition would make it real, "Only you have the power to shape your life and create your happiness…" or something along the lines of "all you need to create your own reality is your mind… Believe in yourself, solve the secret, drink from the holy cup, blah blah blah…" What a ton of horseshit.

He wasn't the master of anything. Which was proven time and time again. He had never been in control of anything in his life, not even his inner world. Always been told how to think, how to behave, how to talk, and how to feel. His father made sure of that.

"Don't even think of crying like a girl! Men don't cry. Real men don't give in to their feelings! You must be tough. I don't ever want to see you like this again, you understand me? Never!"

All the same, he had had a master. One he could neither see nor identify, but was still there. Who or what was it? Was it God? Was it the government? What about his family or society? Maybe a perfect blend of them all? He had no idea. And you can't fight what you can't see. After a time, you stopped even trying to struggle, let alone fight. Then you were ready to lie still in a cage, beaten and consumed; not even tempted to leave by that wide open door. You turned into a circus lion: caged for so long that it's forgotten it was born a predator.

"Are you happy, William? I mean, with your life?" asked Milena.

William was shocked by this question again. This was the second time he was asked if he was happy, by the same person and on the same day. He remembered baring his inner turmoil to Rachel for the first time, spoken about the relentless little soul suckers inside slowly consuming him one bite at a time. He had refrained from using the word "unhappy" but he'd said enough for her to understand that he was.

"William, you have everything most people don't. You have a family, beautiful children and wealth. You shouldn't be like this; you should count your blessings," she had said. Everything that should not be said to someone in depression. It wasn't that she didn't care; she just didn't know any better, she just could never understand. That was the first and last time he had opened up to her. Now with Milena, he had another chance to be understood.

"I am, I guess. Actually, I'm happiest when I hug and kiss my children. And when they look at me eyes full of love and admiration; I find my meaning in being here."

"Why are you afraid of admitting you are not happy, William?"

"I mean, I don't know," William said tentatively. It was clear that he was afraid to confess to something for some reason. Then with a momentous decision, he spilled it all out:

"I guess it's because I was taught I have no right to be unhappy. I should always be thankful to God for everything I have, otherwise, he may punish me by taking them away. And the only thing I'm truly afraid of losing is my children. So I can't be unhappy when I have them or God will punish me."

"Oh, *that* guy again! Phew…" muttered Milena.

"Who?"

"That *God* guy," she replied, "Never mind, we'll come to him soon enough. But for the sake of argument, what would your answer be if there was no God to punish you?"

William sighed deeply, stretching up his upper body and arms. He was like a *truth virgin*, thrilled at the prospect of his first intercourse with total honesty.

"I mean…" he started, "I barely feel anything the whole day and I'm too tired to think when I get to bed. But I know how I feel when I wake up."

"How do you feel when you wake up?"

He froze for a moment. He closed his eyes and gathered courage. Maybe God would forgive him; he was, after all, in a dream. Better yet, if he spoke softly, maybe God wouldn't hear him. It was no mean feat for someone who'd been wearing masks all his life, but as soon as he opened his eyes, he let it all out.

"When I wake up every morning, I feel like putting a fucking gun in my mouth and pulling the trigger," he confessed with an unexpected rush of relief.

"And how does this make you feel?" asked Milena, a surprisingly cool reaction to his frightful confession.

"It… It gives me peace. Like a ton lifted off my shoulders. It feels like freedom," William blurted out. He knew exactly how he felt and longed for that sensation every morning, "Like I'm reaching the end of my meaning in this solid, aimless existence. Once my children are old enough to cope with my untimely death, I don't see any reason to live another day."

"That's the spirit, my boy!" exclaimed Milena, "Now we're rolling. The doors are opening and it's going to flood soon. Excellent! I didn't expect it to be this quick and easy."

William gave a timid smile, "You're glad that I dream of death? How come?"

"Because this proves that you're special, Pups. In your despair and misery, your eyes are open; you're awake. You just don't understand what the hell is happening and why life seemed more and more meaningless as you grew older," she replied, "Your downward spiral to dreams of self-destruction is a gift, believe me. It means that you reject with all your being the dogma they call the system. It means that you want to see, assess and fix whatever is wrong with it. But you, like all other human beings, are being held back by force and fear. Even as you see the truth, malevolent forces curb you by sheer power and spiritual domination, and torture your soul. In the end, you're left with the pre-programmed task designated to you, to you all, to repeat it over and over, until you die." She sounded like an affectionate mother. "A wise man once stated, 'depression is your avatar telling you it's tired of being the character you're trying to play.' This is what this system forces people to become. Some see it and try to fight back, some accept it and get on with the program, some opt out like the way you think of doing, some never see it, some never even care. But all live in denial. In denial that things can change."

Opt out. What a casual and civilized way of saying suicide, thought William.

"As for your God, forget him!" came a throwaway remark from Milena, "This is between you and *them.* God

– or whatever you call it – has no part in this, if it even exists in the first place."

"Oh, you think there's no God then?" asked a defiant William.

"There may be one or not. But if there is one, it certainly is not the way you define it."

"Which is?"

"An all-powerful type, sitting in his throne above the heavens, watching and judging every single one of your acts, and either punishing or rewarding you for them," replied Milena, "What a stupid idea you have reigning supreme over your heads. A vengeful God who casts terrible disasters upon you, judges you for your beliefs, your inner thoughts, your sexual desires and for who you love, how you live. He kills innocent children for no reason and allows wicked people to go on... But guess what, he loves you!" Milena's laughter was more than sarcastic now. "What utter nonsense! And you have no proof of his existence other than a few books which make no sense whatsoever and were written thousands of years ago by people you never saw or met. Fuck this shit! Don't you have any respect for yourself at all?"

"This is exactly what a demon would say to tempt me," he said dubiously.

"Oh, my poor monkey. With all your intellect and endless amount of information to your hand, you still can't figure out the origin of your religions. How afraid they made you of God and hellfire. You've been indoctrinated in implausible stories for more than three thousand years. How are they any different than the fables of Greeks or the Nordics, the tales you call myths? You have no proof for any of it either. Yet you choose to believe in one and reject the others as folk tales. Why? Because *they* chose one for you and programmed you for thousands of years to believe in them."

"You're trying to confuse me with unfounded theories," said William, overwhelmed.

"Come on. That's the best you can do? You know I have a point. What happened to being open-minded?" she countered, "Everything in your holy books was written much earlier on Sumerian clay tablets around 4000 BC. The flood, Adam and Eve, the serpent, the Garden of Eden, the whole nine yards. They were found in their thousands and interpreted. They chronicle events dating back to 400.000 years. And the only thing they never mention? A God. Instead, they talk about gods. Gods that were flesh and blood. They just rehashed everything in those old books, except the made-up bits, of course." Her laugh held that demented note again.

"So what? Everything we have been taught for millennia is a lie?" asked William.

"Hell yes!" she snapped, "Think about it. They got the original account, interpreted and edited the stories to suit them, removed what they didn't want, added some new characters and events and voilà! You got yourself a brand new script. A script which can be used to control the masses and dominate them. The new versions may have made sense to those primitives thousands of years ago, but how do these beliefs shape the world around you today? Can you actually say that these so-called *original books* weren't twisted again and again over centuries to serve the powers that be? Can you honestly say they make the world a better place?"

"Yes, they do. Without religion, people would be killing one another on the spot!" said William confidently.

"And they don't now? You've been killing one another in the name of your gods for thousands of years. The greatest killers among you are those who justify those horrors in the name of their god and religion. If there was really a God, it would be terrified of you, trust me," Milena replied.

"What then, should we get rid of God?"

"Well, maybe. Not necessarily, though. You should start to see God as it is. An unknown power, a mysterious force, not one obsessed with what you do or think. More importantly, though, you should get rid of your outdated and twisted religions," answered Milena and added: "Look, maybe there is a God; I honestly don't know. I've never seen or heard of it. Maybe the universe is God, maybe the whole consciousness of the cosmos is God. The thing is, it doesn't matter if there is one or where he resides or what he thinks. What you should understand is that you no longer need a god. You're spiritually advanced enough to know the difference between good or bad, right or wrong. What you lack is the right intention!"

"What do you mean by intention?" asked William curiously.

"The intention to live for the greater good rather than for individual desire. This is what they fear more than anything; they'll do anything in their power to prevent you from attaining this collective consciousness. Religion is only one of many powerful tools they use to keep you sedated and confused, if not the strongest," Milena explained.

"Tools? What tools?"

"Tools they use to build your cage disguised as *the way of the world*. Money, media, technology, political systems, and, of course, the king of them all, religion. Their goal: control over you, by means of hate, fear, confusion, and ignorance."

"These are well-known facts, Milena," William addressed her by name for the first time, "There's nothing new in what you're telling me. What's the point in arguing about them?"

"There is none," came the adamant reply, "We're not here merely to let off some steam. We are here to find a way to destroy them. But it requires remembering how the system works. So we will talk about them a bit, no more. Remember Sun Tzu: If you know the enemy and know yourself, you need not fear the result of a hundred battles. If you know yourself but not the enemy, for every victory gained you will also suffer a defeat. If you know neither the enemy nor yourself, you will succumb in every battle."

William was impressed and inexplicably, a little aroused too.

"I think we've come far enough to cover the first part, for now. Anyone who can own up to depression and thoughts of suicide surely knows a few things about who he or she is."

"I don't know who I am. I only know I don't belong here or anywhere I know, for that matter," said William, abashed like a child who's just broken a valuable vase.

"You know yourself more than you think, William. You just can't find a way to fit into this pile of stones you call life. Because it is corrupted, disfigured, twisted and chaotic. Just how *they* like it," Milena said, "The truth is, you can't fit a perfect figure into a muddled equation. Even if you did, it still wouldn't mean anything sensible."

"So, what's the solution then?"

"You need to demolish the whole structure and start again with much different priorities and aims. In any everlasting and strong structure, be it a building or a whole new way of life, the foundation is the most crucial bit. This is what I meant by *intention*," Milena explained calmly. She grew more stupendous by the minute. And sexier.

"I love these words, but they too are nothing new. It makes no difference when you have no idea how to do it," said William desperately.

"That's why we are here, William, to create the

foundations of the revolution. But first, let's identify the enemy again. Let's put a face on them. Let's talk about their tools and then unmask them once and for all. And lastly, talk about how to dethrone them. So how about we start with religion first?"

"Haven't we talked about religion already?"

"Yes, but not thoroughly enough. To better understand the enemy, we need to dig into the source of it all," she replied, "Tell me, why do you think people needed religion in the first place? Did they invent it? Or was it already there and they merely discovered it?" Resting her chin on her hands, she gazed into William's eyes. She crossed her knees. She looked just adorable. The pressure of her hands pushed her lips upward.

William felt he was falling in love with butterflies in his stomach and a sweet sensation in his chest. His loins were on fire.

"Well…" he started to speak but stopped.

He was in a trance; the beautiful demon sitting opposite had the face of a barely legal schoolgirl; she was making it hard to think clearly. The blood intended to feed his brain was rushing elsewhere.

"I'm not so sure. We've been taught that faith came naturally to men, as they couldn't ascribe meaning to the greatness of nature or the mysteries above, all the perfect creatures on Earth, everything that surrounds them. So they needed to believe in something much greater than everything and everyone. A supreme creator of all things."

"What you just explained is how God came to be, not religion. I may buy the idea of a supreme creator; hell, I can almost believe there must be one, God or whatever you call it. But you could have stopped there. With God came religion though. Why and how? That was my question," replied Milena. Her hands were no longer under her chin, not that it made her look any less cute.

"I mean, people needed guidance, rules to behave correctly. They weren't as prudent as we are today. So God sent them prophets with his message and list of rules. At least, this is the way it happened in the big three. Some cultures created their own gods in various forms, names and powers. But the ones that concern us at the moment are the current big ones, right? The monotheistic ones?" asked William.

"Yes, they have been the usual suspects for a time now, haven't they?" Milena said with a smile, "So you believe God sent messengers – or prophets as you call them – with a list of to-dos and not to-dos. And told them to warn others; if they don't obey these laws or refuse to believe in him, they will burn in hell for all eternity? Oh, this rule differs a bit in each of them. In one, you burn till the end of eternity. Like eternity having an end makes any sense. In another, you burn until you pay your penance, then go to heaven and party with dozens of beautiful chicks. I don't remember if there's an equivalent for women, though. In short, if you do good, you go to heaven and live happily ever after; if you do bad, you go to hell and are tortured by demons, I mean actual ones, with forks and all, not me; and you're fucked. Is that correct?" Milena asked with a derisive smile on her plump lips.

"In a nutshell, yes..." William was struggling not to laugh out loud. But his eyes were cracking up.

"Hmm and you, after thousands of years and a shit load of scientific advances, still believe it blindly?"

"Well, partying with dozens of girls doesn't sound so bad," William was laughing now.

"Ha-ha-ha, yeah, it does sound good for you; let's ask your wife too, shall we? Nobody mentions parties with dozens of fit hunks, do they?" Milena joined in the laughter.

Were they having fun?

"Yeah, I'm sure she'd want a say in this," said William. Their laughter was fading now.

"It's all make-believe, you know that, right?" Milena was serious now. That absolute control over her sudden change of expression was astonishing. "There's no hell or heaven above. It's all here, in the present realm. You still can't see that heaven or hell is a construct you can apply to your lives, here, on earth. You don't have to wait a lifetime for them. Again, the key is the intention behind your actions."

"I've heard it before. It's really a reassuring idea. But not applicable I'm afraid," said William, "People, how can I put it, can be total assholes. They hate, they get jealous, they fear what they don't understand, harbor all kinds of dogma. They lie for their own benefit, kill for skin color and over someone's sexual preference, betray even their most loved ones and always, always want to dominate. The ego of men knows no bound. I don't see how this bunch can create a heaven on earth."

"You may be right. The question is, why? Why are they this way?" Milena sounded as though she were challenging him this time. She obviously knew the answer; just wanted William to find it on his own.

"It's our nature. It's been in our DNA since the first ape stood up. Kill or be killed. Fear and hate the unknown, so that you can protect your own. What was true in the savannah then still is under the city lights today. So the loop continues. Blood for blood, eye for an eye, destroy what is different, dominate the herd, all's fair to get what you want, the end justifies the means," William replied calmly, although he looked hopeless.

"Fucking everything that breathe and walk are also carved in your DNA. But you don't see people banging one another mindlessly on the streets, do you? So it can be taught, controlled, can't it? Not like you don't have a choice," said Milena.

"Yes, of course. But maybe we don't want to, since it serves our interests and feeds our ego. You can find a hotel room to fuck one another's brains out but once you hate, you cannot contain it. It must be satisfied. And it usually happens instantaneously and in full view. When you get that itch, you need to scratch it at once. Smart people, the big fish do it behind closed doors. They never get their hands dirty. They find someone else to do their dirty work. But the result is always the same. Hate must be satisfied. Either on who caused it or some poor shmuck who had nothing to do with it but was in the wrong place at the wrong time. Once you hate, you must use every means to reach your end. Hate is a powerful mistress; she always gets her way."

"Exactly, William, but the end is also the starting point in this construct. What you believe is a just end is neither just nor good. You believe you hate for good reason, therefore have the right to destroy and dominate because you think you deserve to and it's best for them. But domination is never pure. Neither do the actions to reach that end. And every one of you believes you have a right to rule. Either to rule your wife and children, your co-workers or your society. The most arrogant ones believe they have the right to dominate all of humankind, lead them to greatness and usher in a new era of a perfect world. The quest for domination always begins with hate," she said. Milena's eyes seemed bigger and brighter, "What if the end was to inspire? Would it justify any means then?"

"You can't inspire them all. But you can dominate them all, by force," William replied.

"No, you can't inspire them all, but perhaps just enough to inspire others and spread the word. Sure, it takes longer than dominating but it's certainly much more sustainable and less bloody," said Milena, "Which is where religion comes into play. Their end is not to inspire, not the way they'd intended in the beginning but to dominate, crush dissent, impose their agenda on naïve believers by using God as the enforcer, to rule them all, make them blind slaves who believe this world's pains and sufferings are natural things to be endured. Religion is no more a God-made construct. It's been twisted by men of greed. Greed for power, money and domination. You don't need them any longer. You don't need religion any longer. You need to wake up and see that you are being controlled by malevolent wolves in sheep's clothing, you are being manipulated for their end: accept your fate out of fear of God."

William stayed silent this time. He had no response; he knew it was true.

"What better *hell* can you imagine than the thing you call life today? Constant torture in an unknown hell can't be more delicious than giving a taste of happiness and joy through demagoguery, and so taking whatever you want from people, can it?" Milena continued, "Gods and deities do not run this world, William. Intentions do. It's the intentions that carry energy to shape your reality. You, each one you, are your own god. God is a reflection of your own intentions. The problem is that *they*'ve been manipulating your intentions so that your negative energy can power up their reality. Hate is their bread and butter and you've been feeding them for centuries."

"What then, love is the way, is that what you're saying? Isn't it a bit of a cliché, Milena?" asked William with a sneer.

"Fuck love!" Milena thundered, "The universe doesn't care about love. You don't have to love one another. Love is a luxury, a unique gift for those with the right intentions. All you have to is avoid hate unless there is good reason, and accept one another as equals, whatever your skin color, gender or beliefs."

"So is it OK to hate for a reason?" William was surprised.

"Why not? It's a natural response for humans to hate the people who inflict pain on them. It is OK to hate. You're not ready to be free of it yet; you're not mature enough. Before you are ready, you just need to hate the right people, not the ones you're directed to hate for no good reason. Primarily, not your fellow men. Because if you fall into their scheme and your primitive feelings, if you hate one another on the basis of race, sex, religion, beliefs, and ideas, then you spend it all on trivia and you won't have enough awareness left to see what *they* are doing to you and hate *them* for it. This is the way they operate. Don't feel bad about hate. Even the universe hates disorder and acts ruthlessly to restore balance by destroying things that don't fit," Milena said.

William seemed confused. He was struggling to see the truth about Milena. Was she a manipulator or a holy teacher? What was she?

"I'm what you may call a demon".

William couldn't get her voice out of his skull, those relentlessly repeated words. After her last statement, her voice in his head seemed to rise in pitch. What was she saying? That the three big religions were secretly in league? That they were manipulating their flocks to hate one another to achieve their grand design? Which was what?

As William wrestled with those chaotic thoughts, Milena suddenly let out a demented yell, which made him flinch.

"Money! Yes, goddamn money. Money, money, money… Won't bring happiness but at least you can be miserable in luxury, right?" Milena said, more like teased,

"Another thing you must hate. Another thing that must go."

"Oh, come on!" William protested, "Now we are enemies of capitalism? What, do we need to bring back communism? Unfortunately, money, with all its faults, is a necessary evil. We have tried other ways: they all ended in tyranny and bloodshed."

"Are you aware that in thirty years, eighty percent of today's jobs will be done by robots? Not just the blue collar jobs or hospitality services, but most of the legal and medical services too! What do you think will happen to all those people who'll have no means to earn a crust? I hope you don't expect them to just roll over and die quietly, because they won't. There will be social turmoil all over the world. They will rise up to the unbelievably rich elite. What will happen to your precious capitalism then? You don't need to repeat the same mistakes that proved to be corruptible but you need to find a new system – because this one will fail sooner than later," said Milena.

She carried on before he could think of a smart retort.

"You're a wealthy man, William, are you not?"

"Y-Yes…" William replied shyly.

"And you are neck-deep in depression with plans of suicide, aren't you?"

"I know where you're going with this, Milena," said William with a half-assed smile.

Bowing from the waist, right arm behind her back, left one below her beautifully crafted breasts, Milena said: "I humbly accept your yield…" William felt those butterflies again.

"This doesn't mean we should get rid of money though. What should we replace it with? Barter?" asked William.

"Of course not. You should switch to sharing," answered Milena, not teasing this time.

"Share what with who and to what amount?" asked William, "Why would someone who worked their asses off their whole life share their earnings with others? Why would a genius who invents something that makes millions of people's lives better should share his wealth with others, who contributed nothing to his hard work or his God-given intellect for that matter? We are not created equal, Milena. Some of us are more intelligent than others, better educated, born into better opportunities, better places, or better societies."

"Yeah baby, keep 'em coming darling, you're on fire!" Milena sounded insane again.

"Keep what coming? I'm just making a rational point here. No need to ridicule me."

"Ahem, I'm not, William. I just got carried away, that's all," Milena apologized, "Are you aware that your own words betray the very thing you're trying to justify?"

"Which is what?"

"The inequality of the world born out of mere luck!" Milena answered, "Why must a newborn's fate be sealed from the beginning because of where he or she was born, because of his or her family, because of their intellect? None of these are their choices. They have no control over these conditions. Should they be deprived of warmth, food or a good life just because the dice didn't fall in their favor while they were conceived in their mama's womb? Does luck justify suffering?"

"Ideally, no. It breaks my heart. Unfortunately, that's the way of the world, Milena."

"It should not be, William. There is a way to change this," Milena started to explain, "The resources of the world are more than enough for everyone. They may easily be distributed to the less fortunate. Food, water, shelter, clothing, a free life, access to a good education, and the opportunity to thrive should be everyone's birthright. The thing is, *they* don't want this. A sensible, educated, learned world population is what they loathe. So they distribute the more vital resources in favor of their design, to a select few. They give just enough to the others, who are the majority by the way, to allow them to survive but not to live. They take it back whenever it suits them. This is how they control the game. This is the way they rule."

"Oh, *they* again… Who are they? The priests, imams or rabbis?" William sounded frustrated again.

"Them and more… The royals of the world. The super-rich elite, the patriarchs of faith, the big money dealers, the tyrants of the world…"

"The usual suspects. So what's new?" William hit back.

"Nothing. Remember, we know who they are but do we really know them? We need to dive deeper into their mechanisms so that *we truly know our enemy*," said Milena, "Tell me, can you name one thing in technology that has not been changed or advanced in more than a hundred years? Let me give you a tip. It starts with E."

"I don't know, you tell me," William sighed. He looked bored.

"Energy, William, energy. A hundred and fifty years ago, you were traveling with horses. Now you are working on flying cars and autonomous vehicles. The longest commercial flight takes nineteen hours now and gets shorter by the minute. You're on the verge of genetically designing humans, creating artificial intelligence and artificial realities. Hell, you're making solid plans to create colonies on other planets and working on solving the secrets of creation. And you did all this in just fifty years. Yet you still rely on subterranean fossil fuels and gasses; that's been the norm for more than a hundred years. Everything advances, except energy sources. Why do you think that is?" asked Milena, daring him to think deeper.

"Because they haven't found an alternative yet. Not one that's efficient enough, at least," said William, accepting the challenge.

"Haven't they? Are you sure? Greater advances were made in science. Except for any feasible alternative to energy. Isn't this a little bit suspicious?" Milena continued to dare.

"What would be the point of hiding something like this, Milena? Every scientific advance is shared with the public, yet they choose to shelve the next phase in energy? To what end?"

"Because, William, the next phase is free energy. Do you honestly believe that no one hasn't already discovered to obtain unlimited and free energy? You're about to find the so-called God Particle, for crying out loud! You're about to set off for other planets, build homes and live there! Yet you still have no alternative to trees and dinosaur shit from millions of years ago? No technological or scientific advancement, with all your might and your intellect, to replace goddamn fossils and break humankind's dependence on a group of cowboys and Bedouin? Oh, let's not forget the vodka lovers," Milena burst out laughing.

"How can someone contain this kind of knowledge in the internet age? Someone would surely share it on the net, even if it was classified or buried deep within some black-budget agency archives, someone would leak it. It just doesn't make sense."

"They've already done it, and countless times too! Only to be ridiculed by the mainstream media and scholars, suppressed and intimidated by dark figures. Some even died in very mysterious ways. Hell, Thomas Edison did it to Nikola Tesla a hundred years ago, and the perp has been imposed on every school child as a hero," said Milena, "Did you know that every big oil company has been derived from one giant company, and that they're also the majority owners of the biggest banks in the world, including the central banks? Oh, and the biggest shareholders in big pharma too," Milena seemed more than angry now.

William thought she looked even sexier when angry.

"Ooh! We have a conspiracy theory; how exciting!" he said, eyes flashing with mockery. He was having fun. But it was not to last.

"This is no joke, William!" Milena's sudden roar shook him to the bone. She got up and strode towards him.

Her face, William heard his own scared inner voice, *It's no longer human…*

The yellow of the iris had spread to the whole of the eyes. Her cheekbones looked much sharper than before; her once perfect teeth now sported two fangs and claws had replaced those elegant long fingers.

That transition took no more than a few seconds before William's eyes; his synapses captured those images, dispatched them to his brain and labeled them – but it wasn't long enough to process it all. So his good old instinct kicked in: fight or flight…

With no time to even choose, all he could manage was a rather pathetic *"AIIIEEEE! Christ, what the hell is going on?"*

"You're not taking this seriously enough, William!" growled Milena. It wasn't just her face and hands that had changed; she now sounded like a monster. A legion was speaking out of her now. "You have to understand your situation and dedicate yourself to the task ahead! But you still act like a child. Think this is some brainstorming session? If you don't devote yourself to your calling and act on it, you will be annihilated, all of you! Do you think this is a game? You will perish; you'll all die such gory deaths to put those 'eighties slashers into the shade. Your flesh and blood will feed the earth below, the very same earth you destroy on a daily basis with your fucking oil,

500 hp cars, airplanes, coal, and toxic wastes. You will beg for a mercy killing! Your agony and your suffering will be legendary, even in your hell!"

William remained frozen, his face a blend of fear, shock and terror.

"But maybe that's what you need," Milena continued, "Maybe you need to suffer to appreciate how crucial this is. You've been living in a golden cage for so long that the way of the world is merely a brandy room conversation for you. A trivial topic that makes you feel important, to show what a fucking intellectual you are to your pathetic holier-than-thou friends. The topics of your arrogant debates with those privileged senators' sons, however, mean actual pain and suffering for the majority in the world."

Milena's face was returning to normal as her voice was softened from that growl. She walked back and sat on the peak of a dust hill again. She looked a little calmer.

"Yes, I know what your medicine is, William. You've been taking the blue pill for so long. It's time to take the red one," Milena said, looking up, "Yes, we need to bring forth the empath in you. And the path to true empathy is paved with stones of pain. So, shall we begin in earnest now?"

She stood up again, walked towards a trembling William and placed her right hand on his left shoulder. Stunned by a blinding flash and vibration, he sensed that same emptiness he felt on the bench where he had met Milena for the first time.

CHAPTER 3
BEATI
QUI SUFFERUNT

O, the suffering, the sweet suffering.
Come to me and cleanse the filth out of my soul.
Purify me with your whip and lick my wounds with your
venom.
Only through you will the Sun shine upon the truth.
Only through you will the strength to cast evil embrace me.
O, the suffering, the sweet suffering…
How terrible and beautiful you are…

William woke up in darkness. He was soaking wet, lying down with his head on Milena's lap. She was caressing his hair. It was pitch black. There was nothing to see, not even an obscure shape. Except for their reflection gently waving on the surface of water an inch deep. He couldn't identify the source of the light – until his gaze fell on Milena's bare legs. They glowed, as did the rest of her body. He felt paralyzed, faint. Her tender fingers continued to stroke his hair up and down.

His heart was pounding hard enough to be heard. He wanted to scream but his voice was gone. He wanted to cry but wasn't calm enough to do it. He was aroused by those glossy long legs. The scent of her poreless skin made him giddy. Her warmth was like nothing he'd ever known.

He felt as though he'd just fused with her every molecule. He wanted to devour that flesh, be one with her.

What kind of a man could think about sex at a moment like this? he thought, disgusted with himself. How could he get aroused now? How?

"You little bastard, how can you be such a filthy boy? Turn it off at once, you pervert! And lock yourself in the bathroom! Don't get out of there till I say you can!"

The memory of his father's shout took him back to the time when he was caught watching a passionate French kiss in a movie.

"Shut up, you monster, you're dead!" he shouted back in his mind.

The monster's bellow faded away at Milena's gentle voice.

"This is the first and last caress you will get from me, William. Your holy pilgrimage begins now. You will have firsthand experience of the horrors caused by the order of this world. Horrors many of your fellow men were subjected to. You will feel things. Things you've only half heard between the headlines on late-night TV news. Your body and soul will be crushed. You will dance on the edge of madness. But in the end, you will come out the other side, born anew. Born wiser, stronger and holier. Have faith, have courage. This is your moment of truth. Embrace it with all your heart," Milena whispered in his ear.

Her warm breath was comforting. William wanted to respond somehow. But his mouth still couldn't move.

"Look into the emptiness one last time, William. Our sacred journey is at hand. Rejoice: you will come out the other side blessed."

William raised his head from her lap slowly. He was no longer paralyzed. Losing contact with her skin was like leaving a warm house to walk barefoot on ice. He looked around the black void. It made him feel at home.

Then came that flash of light and feeling of nothingness again.

Part 1 – Thou Shalt Not

Louis got out of bed at around 6.30. Dressed calmly, walked straight to the bathroom, went in, and shut the door. He peed, washed his face with cold water, wet his hair, and combed it. The mirror reflected his sunken dark eyes. He hadn't slept a wink. He hadn't watched TV or listened to music. All he had done was lie in bed and stare up at the ceiling. The face in the mirror looked eerie. Pinching himself and roaring in silence through his teeth, he was headbanging as if in a death metal concert.

After five minutes or so, he got out and headed to Thea's room. Cautiously pushing all the way the half-open door, he looked in. He watched his sister for a few minutes. The poster hanging above the bed was barely visible but he knew what it was. It was he who had given it to her about a year ago, after all.

"What are you listening to, Louis?" Thea had asked then.

"It's Slipknot, a hardcore rock band. You wouldn't like it."

"Let me listen."

"Get lost Thea, the best part is coming."

"Come on, let me hear it, Louis, please," Thea had asked with her palms pressed together as if in prayer. Louis had found it sweet and silly.

"All right; but just for a minute, I need to listen to it with both ears, you know."

"Yay!"

Looking at the poster, he remembered that as soon as she had heard it, she was in love. He couldn't have shooed her even if he'd tried. So he had caved in, let her stay and they had listened to the hardcore band all night long. It was surprising that she'd enjoyed such heavy music, *It must be a phase*, he had thought: he had never known a girl to like Slipknot, only maggots like himself.

It was a good memory.

Slowly pulled the door back without shutting, he headed to his parents' room.

He watched them for a little longer than he did his sister. His mother was sleeping with her mouth wide open. *Sleep makes even the most beautiful woman look like an idiot*, he thought.

His father was snoring. Such a funny sound from that serious man. How vulnerable he looked even as he made those bestial noises. With a half-smile and another look at his mother, Louis pulled the door, again without shutting it fully. It would have made a noise and wakened them.

Walking down the stairs silently, he took his knee-long coat from the hanger and walked out of the door before putting it on. He may have been in a hurry, but he still had to move like a mouse. He shut the door softly, being extra careful with the click, as the lock was noisier than a standard one. On reaching the sidewalk, he turned back. Took a good look at his house. The front yard where they'd had birthday parties and played fantasy games when he was a kid looked much smaller than he remembered.

"Daddy! Let's play animalism!" he remembered saying when he was six years old. Animalism: what a childish name for a game where people pretend to be animals. His favorite was *tigerism*.

"You're the daddy tiger, I'm the baby tiger, come on dad!"

He was lost in that memory when a drop of rain tickled down the back of his neck. He didn't care. He wanted to stay in that lost moment.

With a deep sigh, he turned left, stopped after a few steps and turned his upper body to take another look at his home, turned back to the street again and continued to walk.

As he carried on the wet sidewalk, he looked up at the sky. It was raining but it was not dark. It was greenish. The winter sun had not risen yet but its light was already shining on the clouds. He couldn't understand why it was green. He was disappointed. He had wanted to see blue sky, especially that morning.

He walked through the streets aimlessly for a while. Then he stopped and looked up to the sky again. It was still green, with a hint of red now. Still no hint of blue, "Why is it raining today of all days..." he murmured. He had really hoped to see blue sky.

After a while, his steps took a clearer direction towards the infamous northern side of the city. The part where every crook, pimp and criminal called home. His mother had once driven him through it to avoid a traffic jam. She'd been freaked out by the kind of guys knocking on their windows. He was around fourteen then, a tough guy, he had thought. A side effect of adolescence. That illusion had gone up in smoke when a junkie had banged his head at the front window and flashed a gun. He was mumbling something but there was no way they could make it out. Possibly asking for money. It had never occurred to Louis that in his mother's hands, that fifteen-year-old Citroen Saxo could turn into a race car. They had both looked back to see if they'd run over the guy. And never drove through that shithole again.

But Louis had been seen there for some time now. An old school friend, a guy called Valentin had run into him on the street a few weeks ago. Once a successful and well-behaved student, Valentin had changed around two years ago after meeting Chloe at a local mall. Chloe was best described as a troublemaker. She was a raw anarchist, a ferocious liberal and a crack addict. Also beautiful and extremely self-confident. Valentin had been the perfect sucker. He was handsome, naïve and best of all, oppressed his whole life; hungry for the pleasures he had been denied. It had all happened really quickly. Within a few weeks, Valentin had transformed himself into a punk. Next, he had rebelled against the school authority. His parents had been informed about his transformation when Chloe had shown up at the school gate one day and they had left together grabbing each other's asses. Father Emmanuel (who had baptized Louis, and was his father's best friend to boot) had called Valentin's parents straightaway.

Valentin burned his bridges when he gave Father Emmanuel the middle finger in front of the students at lunchtime. It had begun with Father Emmanuel telling him to have his hair trimmed to the school's standards, that he looked like a terrorist. Instead of saying yes, Valentin had surprised his schoolmates by taking two slow steps back, putting his middle finger in his mouth, moaning as he sucked on it for a few seconds, taking it out and pointing it at Father Emmanuel with a wicked grin.

Everyone, including Louis, had struggled to stop themselves from cheering and whistling. Father Emmanuel had never looked more helpless. Valentin had become a legend from that moment on. Needless to say, he was expelled and had a massive row with his parents at home. Louis had later heard that he had left home to live with Chloe. That was the last he'd heard of Valentin. Until two weeks ago.

When he had spotted Valentin sitting on the steps of an old building together with some creepy guys. He had looked quite different from that day at school. His hair was much longer, with the sides shaved; his nose and lip sported several piercings, and he was dressed in black from top to toe. The pallor of his face suggested a ton of white powder, although it was natural. Valentin had looked ten years older, much thinner, yet happy.

Louis had considered changing direction but Valentin had already locked his narrowed eyes on him. It was too late.

"Louis? Is that you?" Valentin had yelled.

"Ye-Yes?" Louis had pretended he hadn't recognized him.

"Holy shit! It's me, Valentin, your old school pal. You remember me, right?"

"Oh, of course, Valentin; Christ! It's been ages, how are you?" Louis had asked walking towards him. One single word rang in his mind. *Fuck! Fuck, fuck!*

"Man, how long's it been since we last saw each other, three, four years?" Valentin had asked, already up and about to give him a hug. Louis' attempt to avoid it politely (standing with his arms crossed) had made no difference: he got a hug anyway. Louis, like the gentleman he was raised, had hugged back reluctantly.

"It's only been two years since you left," Louis had corrected Valentin's memory.

"Yeah, you may be right. Life is much slower here."

"Actually, same there too."

"What are you up to, man? Still attending that holy prison?"

"Unfortunately, yes."

"Damn, how can you still stand those hypocrites?"

"No choice. Not for much longer now, though. I only have a year to go."

"Shit, it's so good to see you. You were one of the good ones, you know. I always liked you," Valentin had said with a smile.

"Thanks, buddy, same here. I was sorry to see you go. You know you're a legend there now?"

"Yeah, right. Someone had to do it years before

my little performance. No regrets," Valentin had said confidently.

"So how are you; what are you up to? Still with that girl, I can't remember her name?" Louis had asked insincerely. He had known exactly what she was called, but had no wish to get too cozy.

"Chloe. Yeah, no man, we broke up about a year ago. I'm living the dream now. Free to do anything anytime I want," Valentin had answered with no hint of sadness.

"I'm sorry to hear about that. Not the dream part, of course, about Chloe."

"Don't be, man, it wasn't meant to be."

"Whatever you say," Louis had said, trying to cut the conversation as short as possible. To no avail.

"I'm so much better without her, man. She was just too possessive. Once you start flapping your wings, any weight that's trying to pull you down grates on the nerves, yeah?"

Louis had got the point, even if he himself could never flap his own wings.

"Say, have you heard anything about my parents, Louis?" Valentin had asked much more seriously this time. It was like he was afraid of the answer.

"Just one time. I heard they moved uptown. Nothing more," Louis had lied once again; he had actually heard that they'd broken up. Their marriage had cracked when their only child had up and left. But he'd noticed the fear in Valentin's eyes; that show of no regrets had failed to conceal his expression. Valentin had been missing them.

"Right, right. Well, what the hell are you doing around this part of the city, Louis? This isn't your usual scene."

Shit, I had no time to come up with an excuse. What should I say? What if he sees someone from school and tells them about me? Damn it; Louis, think fast, think fast!

"I was just strolling to clear my head. I'm a little nervous about college applications. Once I started walking,

I lost track of where I was going and found myself here," he had explained. Louis had found he was becoming an expert in lying on the spot. For a boy who had been raised never to lie, it was impressive, a twisted cause for pride.

"Yeah, I got you, pal. You have your whole life ahead of you. Responsibilities and all, right? Well, good luck to you, I wish all the best to you, Louis, you're a good guy," Valentin had said warmly. That degree of niceness was surprising, especially coming from a guy who looked like a satanist on crack.

"Thank you, Valentin, I wish you all the best too. Well, it's getting late, I better get going."

"Sure, sure. Say hello to our old friends for me, will you?"

"Sure. Take care, Valentin," Louis had said and Valentin had hugged him again. Louis had kept walking until turning into the other street, where he had stood for a while, trying to figure out how to get to where he was going without running into Valentin again. Once that was done, he had never used that old route and never seen Valentin again. Although Valentin did cross his mind from time to time. How the hell did he live? How did he earn a living? Was he really as happy as he claimed to be? Whatever; he wasn't going to blow his mind on these questions: he had his own to answer.

He had been frequenting that neighborhood almost every single day for months now. What business he could have had in that godforsaken hole was anybody's guess, least of all his unaware family's.

That morning, when he had left home around 6.45, it had taken him half an hour to reach his destination. Despite the cold, he still hadn't put his coat on. He stopped in front of a seven-story apartment building. Rang the bell of the fourth floor. While he waited anxiously, he was being watched by a beautiful red-hair in a black leather jacket and a man in a suit across the road. The man, who looked like he came out of a bar after a boozing and debauching the night, was gaping at Louis.

"Is that my son? Is that Charlie?" asked William. He was trying to speak plainly but his voice was trembling.

"Well, yes and no, William. That's your son all right. But he is not Charlie. He is Louis. He lives in Paris with his parents and little sister. He has been attending a Catholic school since he was seven years old. He is seventeen now."

Louis was still waiting to be buzzed in. He was saying something to whoever was at the other end. William couldn't catch any of the words although he could have sworn it wasn't French. Not that he spoke French, but he'd certainly recognize it.

"I don't get it," he pleaded, "If he isn't Charlie, how come he's my son? And my son's only twelve."

"This is one of the countless probabilities that could have been, William. In this one, you were born to a poor family in France, scraped through high school, got married, had children young and lived with your family in a modest three-room house, working as a maintenance manager in a small auto shop," Milena was talking without taking her eye off the boy, who was now buzzed in, "You and your family are devout Catholics. So much so, you sent your children to a Catholic school on the advice of your priest, who happens to be a senior teacher there. And is also one of your best friends. You spend all your Sundays with him. Starting from morning Mass till Sunday night dinner at your home. He baptized both your children."

"I have no recollection of anything you mention," said William.

"Yes, I know. Let's fix that, shall we?" Milena said, placing her hand on his forehead. A thunderbolt cracked in his head. It was like his head had collapsed into itself and a black hole had opened. The images flooding into his mind made him forget who he was for a moment. It took only a few seconds but it was more than enough to knock him to the ground, knock him down hard. Milena smiled at hearing his moans.

"I remember…" whispered William instinctively, "I remember everything…"

"Good… We can go on, then," Milena said, unconcerned.

"Louis is my son. Margaux's my wife. Thea's my daughter. And I am Gabriel…" murmured William.

"Good, good… Very good. Any idea why your son sneaked out much earlier than usual to come to this hellhole?" asked Milena.

"No idea. But he has been acting strange for a few months now. Holy shit, how do I remember this?" William moaned again. The new memories in his mind were crashing into the old ones. It was painful and confusing.

"Hmm, why can it be, why can it be?" Milena said in a childish voice.

"I don't know, all right? I don't know!" a desperate William exclaimed, "He's been coming home late, only to lock himself up in his room and chat online for hours on end. I thought it might be a girl… Ahh!" A pained shout. His mind was tortured by every new memory.

"Anything else seemed weird lately? Like, maybe his church attendance on Sundays?"

"Yes, yes; but he is a teenager, that's normal. He'd not been into religion since he was twelve, anyway. It's a phase, nothing to be concerned about. Happens to us all. His faith has been firm since he was a little boy," William answered. Or maybe Gabriel did. He couldn't tell the difference. Remembering another life was anguish.

"If you say so. What about his mood? Did he seem as cheerful as when he was a kid?"

"I, I don't know. Oh, these memories are killing me. Every time you ask for a detail, my mind tries to enter that memory all by itself. And it hurts, so fucking much!" William moaned again, longer this time. He looked at Milena with the expression of a man who was being beaten within an inch of his life. "For God's sake... Of course, he wasn't as cheerful... He was a teenager; he'd entered puberty. That's when kids tend to get depressed. That's how it is. Why are you asking me all these questions, Milena? Just say what's on your mind. Stop making me remember!" he demanded.

"Fine, I will. It wasn't only puberty that caused his depression. He tried to talk to you a few times. In these exact words:" Milena started to talk in Louis's voice but in French. Somehow, William understood every word. It was strange, hearing his son's voice through Milena's lips in another language. It also made him remember the actual conversation. Another memory, another agony.

"Dad, can I talk to you about something?"

"Sure, Louis, of course. What is it?" Milena said, this time speaking in Gabriel's voice (or was it William's?).

"I want to go to a regular school, papa. I'm not happy there. I want a more open-minded environment," Louis said. (or was it Charlie's voice? It was getting more confusing by the minute.)

"Oh, no, no, no, son. I don't trust public schools. They're not the best choice for a good Christian education. Graduates of those schools are morally corrupt. Trust me, you don't want to lose your faith just because you want more fun. Sorry, but the answer is no."

"But papa, I really am not happy there. I feel suffocated. I don't want to be there. I hate my teachers. Please papa, let me go to a regular school. I won't lose my faith, I promise..." begged Louis.

"I said no!" Gabriel exploded, "I will not allow my thirteen-year-old son to be corrupted by that abomination called modern education. No, sir... "

"Papa, please, hear me out, I hate it there…"

"This conversation is over!" shouted Gabriel.

That last "over" came in Milena's own voice.

William recalled not just the incident but the emotions too. It was strange. He felt Gabriel's fury alongside his own pity for the boy. It was so muddling and bizarre.

He also remembered Louis's hesitation and conflicted expression. It was like the boy was disputing a decision with himself.

"Papa… There is something else I want to…" he began and was interrupted Gabriel's high-pitched roar:

"Louis, enough!"

William remembered Louis's disappointment and fear. *How come Gabriel didn't see it?* he wondered.

"I remember this conversation but how can I be responsible for it? It was not really me deciding his future, it was Gabriel… But I remember, I remember the slightest thing Gabriel felt. I feel it too," said William.

"Do you also remember how many times Louis asked the same question over the years?"

"A few more times…" William confessed. How could he have been feeling guilty about something he had not done. Was it really him who was guilty? Bricks of sorrow and regret weighed down his shoulders.

"How did you respond each time?"

"I said no. I mean he did. This is so baffling," said William, his head bowed.

"Yes, you did, sir. That you did…" Milena said.

"But it wasn't me. I never turned my own Charlie back when he had a problem. It wasn't me," William lifted his head, his eyes open. As if he was trying to clear himself of something bad he had done when he was blind drunk.

"It doesn't matter, Pups. What matters is you feel everything Gabriel has done, looking through Gabriel's eyes. And you will continue to do so in the coming hours too. You two occupy the same mind now. It's like driving a car with two steering wheels, isn't it?"

"So what's the lesson here? Religious guys don't care about their kids' feelings or desires? Is that it?" asked William.

"Oh, no. The lesson is yet to come, William. Be patient. Nothing worth learning comes easy," answered Milena, before pointing to Louis: "Hey, look who's coming out of the door!"

The boy was wearing his long coat. He looked pale.

"Let's see where he's headed."

Louis reached the sidewalk and started walking south. William and Milena followed, ten steps behind him.

"What if he sees me?" asked William.

"He can't see you. Nobody can. Don't worry. You're not here to be seen or interfere with anything. You're here to experience, to feel."

It took half an hour again to reach their home neighborhood. It was around 7.45 now. The sun was up but it was still raining. On the way, Louis stopped a few times and looked up at the sky. William noticed it but chose to ignore it.

Louis took a left before reaching home. William thought he knew where he was going but his mind was so blurred, he couldn't remember where.

Louis walked for another mile before taking a right to get to the street where his school was. He was grabbing his coat's lower lapels like protection from a non-existent wind. It had stopped raining a few minutes back. He looked up one more time and sighed: the sun was still hidden. He entered through the gate; instead of walking up the stairs towards the classrooms section, he walked around the back to the chapel. This was where all teachers and students attended morning prayers. Attendance was mandatory at the thirty-minute assembly. Everyone had to be present by five minutes before the sermon, which always started at 8.00 a.m. sharp.

Louis entered the chapel at 7.53. The house of God was nearly full. Leaning back against the wall by the door, he waited, coat still buttoned up.

William and Milena followed him in fifteen seconds later.

"Can we stand next to him?" asked William.

"Of course; remember, we are invisible."

They approached Louis. William was briefly tempted to talk to the boy – his son, after all. Looked him from head to toe, *He's so big*, he thought; that's how his Charlie would look in five years, *What a handsome devil*. William felt a strange pride. His musings were disrupted by a boy who came over to talk to Louis.

"Hey Louis, good morning. We miss you at the club; how come you quit?" It was Mathis, a friend from the Drama Club.

Louis was a gifted actor; everyone said so. He had joined the club at thirteen and had quickly shined among the more mediocre members. Since then, he had taken the lead in over ten shows, which were all about biblical events. He had never regarded them as real events though; they were just good stories with a lot of fantastic elements. Good for show, bad for real life. For a time, he had enjoyed the stage, even considered going pro after graduation. His father was instantly against the idea: "Acting is for degenerates and atheists!" Not a remark that Louis had minded all that much; he'd be an adult after graduation and do what he wanted.

About a year ago, however, he had left the club in a decision apparently out of nowhere. He never explained why, not that his father asked. He was glad his son had found the right path and would no longer be mingling with the scum of the world.

That was the time when Louis had started to spend time in Valentin's neighborhood after school.

"I got tired of playing in those dumb scripts, Mathis. Why would you miss me anyway? I heard you get the leads now; surely that was what you always wanted?"

"They're not dumb scripts; how can you say something like that about the holy scriptures?"

"Holy, my ass!" mocked Louis.

"Blasphemy! Take it back or I'll tell Father Emmanuel!" exclaimed Mathis.

"Go fuck yourself, Mathis!"

The boy couldn't believe his ears: Louis swore in God's house! *He'll go to hell for this*, he thought, eyes wide open but unable to reply. Hearing him breathe through the nose gave Louis a strange satisfaction.

Mathis turned back to head for the pews.

"Yeah, go be a little lamb now," Louis said behind him, "And don't forget to suck his dick!"

Mathis paused, then carried on without turning back or saying anything. The priest he tried to talk to on the way had his hands full with herding the younger children who were running around like drunken monkeys.

The behavior of this alternate son was unsettling. William's own Charlie would never have talked like that, let alone be that hateful.

"Why is he like that? I remember him being distant and a little rebellious at home but never like this." Efforts to remember more about Louis only brought back the nails hammering into his head.

"Your Charlie never had to go through what poor Louis did. Anyone can be anything. It all depends on the circumstances of their lives."

William didn't like the answer.

"All right, everybody, move to your designated pews and sit down. The sermon will begin in three minutes," the Headmaster spoke into the microphone.

All the pupils between seven and twelve scrambled to their seats. The older ones displayed their relative maturity by adopting a more dignified pace. The only one who did not move was Louis. He waited patiently. A teacher passing by warned him to take his place.

"Just a minute, sister," said Louis, looking and sounding cool as a cucumber, as the kids would say.

"Very well; I believe we are ready for morning prayers," said the Headmaster. He didn't notice the cool boy still standing against the wall.

Just when William was wondering why Louis was still there standing like the anti-hero detective of a crime movie, Louis slowly started to walk towards the aisle. He was still grabbing his lapels.

"Fathers, sisters, hypocrites of the eighth circle of hell, hear me now!" he yelled.

"What's happening?" asked William.

"You'll see. Be patient, Pups," Milena answered.

"You have tricked the innocent for far too long; you have sinned in God's name for so long. You hid your tumors of lust and heresy under your cloaks. But now, it is high time you paid for your transgressions," Louis kept shouting, with not a smidgen of fear in his voice, only hatred and resolve.

"Louis? What are you doing, my son? What's this all about?" the Headmaster asked.

"This is your reckoning, Father, from which no penance can save you. Your punishment and my gift to the world. No more will you poison the young with your atrocities!" Louis answered back in a shout.

"Milena, what's going on? What's he doing?" asked William anxiously.

"Wait, the best part is just coming..." Milena answered with a smile, staring at Louis.

Louis reached the middle of the aisle and threw open

his arms. The jangle of torn buttons falling to the floor echoed on the high walls. A set-up of small boxes and colorful flexes attached to his chest were revealed to the school's full complement.

"Bomb, it's a bomb!" screeched a girl in an aisle seat just in front of Louis. Yells and screams rose up. No one knew what to do, though; they all waited for the instructions from the Headmaster, like the good sheep they were. William was frozen in shock.

"Louis, my son, what are you…"

Louis roared, cutting the Headmaster's words like a knife:

"This is for you, Father Emmanuel!"

The flash of light reminded William of the moments Milena transported him from one place to another in an instant. The only difference was, this was much noisier and more vivid and he wasn't going anywhere. A number of wet and splashy things flew through his body, although in all that dust, it was impossible to see what they were.

Moments later, the dust settled a little and he caught sight of a figure lying a few feet away. He knew it was a human shape. His brain finally made the connection. There was an explosion and his seventeen-year-old son was the bomb.

"Oh my God, Charlie!" William cried out. At a time of danger and panic, he spoke his real son's name. He couldn't hear another single noise, not even the echo of his own voice. Rushing over to the body, he was horrified by the sight: two legs and half a torso severed below the chest. It was like a mannequin's lower body. The only difference was the belly. He was about to yell "Louis!" when he spotted a mark on the torso. A mole, just above the belly button, slightly to the left. He knew that mole. It was not there when the now mutilated body was born. He should have known; it was he who had cut the cord. It was the most magical moment of his life, the moment he always regarded as his meaning in this world, the purest and happiest moment of his whole life. The mole appeared when Charlie was around six.

That mole was their play button for a time bomb. When he pressed it, the bomb would start a beeping countdown from ten. The moment it reached zero, father and son would imitate the *crump* of an explosion and break down in giggles. In William's mind, those laughs had defined what heaven would have been like. It was love in its purest form. He remembered this as both William and Gabriel. What were the odds both fathers had played the same game with their sons?

"Oh, nooo, Louis, my son!!" he was wailing for Louis this time, a cry that upset even Milena, "No, no, no, no… This is not happening, no, God please no… !" All those times his son hugged him, slept on his chest when he was a baby, all those terrified times William woke up at three to check if he was breathing, all the joy, the smiles, the first mumbled sweet words flashed before his eyes. He wanted to reach out and catch them as they passed by all at the same time. Not just William's but Gabriel's too. Double the father, double the grief.

His cries must have been heard from heaven. Maybe it was because there were two sobbing fathers. William couldn't distinguish between Gabriel's sorrow and his own. His head was spinning, his heart was shattering, he felt like he was nowhere, in no time, and was no one…

Looking up at Milena, "My boy, my sweet boy… Why, why?" he squealed, still kneeling beside the torso. He tried to hold it but his hands passed through it.

'Think back to his last moments, William; I'm sure you will figure out why,' she replied gravely.

He was in no state to think back to even a few seconds. All of Louis' childhood memories were rushing into his mind alongside those of Charlie's. He was in too much pain to feel anything other than fear. As he looked around, hoping this was a nightmare and he'd soon wake up, the dust and smoke settled, revealing dozens of bodies on the floor. Men, women and children of all ages. A scene straight of the horror movies he'd loved as a teenager.

"I don't remember, he was cursing the priests, babbling about hell and sin… Oh my God…"

"Think harder, William. Remember his exact words," Milena pressed.

"He said something about Father Emmanuel…" William said hoarsely, "He said 'this is for you, Father Emmanuel'…" His face was covered in tears and slime.

"Your best friend and beloved priest. What could he have to do with it, I wonder?"

"I don't know; I don't know anything. I feel like I'm losing my mind. Is my son alive or dead? Why is this happening; why are you doing this to me?" sobbed William. He had never felt so helpless before.

"Losing your mind already? Come on, grow a pair, William. I have so many more sights to show you… This is just the beginning, Pups."

"No, no, I can't take more of this, release me, I'm not what you think I am… I want to get back, please, take me back…" William begged.

Milena found his misery revolting. "Don't take your eye off the ball, William."

Mark had said the same thing about their big project. How insignificant it seemed now.

"Get a hold of yourself. Why did Louis mention Father Emmanuel? What possible reason could he have had to address him in his last breath? Think, William, think!"

"Fuck you and fuck your fucking task… I don't care, OK?! My son just blew himself up in the where chapel he grew up, with two hundred other children, men and women. What kind of a lesson d'you want me to take from this, you fucking evil demon!" William's fury now overshadowed his sobs.

"That's right! Get mad, rebel, shout, curse! That's the spirit I want. Demand answers, find out the truth behind the charade," Milena said, "Why did this happen? Do you want to get to the bottom of the truth or do you want to sob like a child?"

"Why, tell me, stop the bullshit! Yes, I want to know why!"

"Sure; I'll tell you why," Milena started to explain, "This happened because your faith in your so-called holy friend made you deaf to your son's cries for help. Your precious Father Emmanuel had been raping your son for three years starting from the age of twelve. He told him he was transferring God's love through his sacred body. He used God to justify his own wicked perversion and terrify Louis into silence. That's why he wanted to move to a public school. That's why he was estranged from the church and your God. That's why, when he met a radical Islamic terrorist group to buy a gun, their promise for revenge suited him like a glove, suited his abused and angry soul. They brainwashed him into believing that his act would punish the wicked and spare other innocents. At first, he resisted. His original idea was to only kill Emmanuel and then kill himself. He had no intention to harm the innocent. But they succeeded in convincing him that by killing them all, he would be saving the innocent and they would go to heaven. He didn't care about the heaven remark, as he had already lost his faith at that point. But he was terrified by the thought of other small boys suffering the same nightmare. Sparing them by killing them all would be an act of mercy and also send a message to all the other so-called holies that the same thing could happen to them. Irrational and deceptive as it was, repeated with systematic flattery and proven methods of inculcation, the idea did eventually make sense to him. Louis truly believed that he was doing something right and saving the innocent. Those radicals, in the meantime, knew that a dead clergyman and a boy's suicide wouldn't have grabbed as much attention as a massacre in a church full of children, that's why they insisted on something on this scale. This is why religion had been called the opium of the masses. At its core, it is the ultimate weapon for destroying common sense. Louis hated religion and Father Emmanuel along with everything he represents; add to that his father's betrayal and he was the perfect candidate for those radicals' maniacal aims. A suicidal boy longing for revenge and justice, ready to be used to spread their heinous message through terror, just like the thousands of other boys who had done similar things disguised under a holy reason; in reality, nothing more than terror in the name of hate. A hate sowed in Louis by the false holiness of one faith and harvested by another. Perfect alliance for a catastrophe. Once they had put their hooks in him, it was over before it started."

"No, it can't be. You're lying to me, you're manipulating me. Emmanuel would never do that! He's a good man, a good Christian! You're lying!" exclaimed William, remembering his dear friend. Pain laid over pain was becoming maddening.

"Let's say I am; what about your son? Was he lying too?" asked Milena and carried on, "The devil always speaks in the sweetest voice. He sells you dreams of heaven in exchange for your ignorance and blindness. He suckles on your faith and devours your soul. He usurps angels and smite you with aches for your flesh while pretending to save your soul. And you, in all your ignorance, accept his minions disguised in holy cloaks as your medium between God and you, as you need someone to comfort you in believing there is one after all."

Looking deep into William's tearful eyes, she continued: "Holy father, huh? What kind of idiots are you? How is he holy, when he is only flesh and blood, just like you? What miracle has he performed to be called holy? Other than memorizing a book. You crown your own oppressors in the name of someone you never saw and have no proof of, just to persuade yourself of your God's existence." Milena held William's face between her hands and came a little closer. Too close to be seen clearly now.

"Did you know that millions of children are abused in the world every year? Not all by priests of course. Devils are everywhere... But more than half of these children are abused by religious figureheads, priests, imams, sheiks, rabbis, and so on and so forth. Not all clerics are abusers, obviously, there are a lot of true believers, good people among them too. But you can't deny that a holy hat helps cover the tracks of evil more than any other profession, just like the way it was with you, isn't that right, my sweet William – or should I call you Gabriel yet? We will dive deeper into this lesson later. For now, I hope you get the main idea."

"I don't know what to think. I don't even know what I know. Please, I don't want to be here anymore... Please, I beg of you, take me back..."

"Where do you want to go, William?"

"Home, I want to get back to my home. To my real family, to my real world. Please, end this nightmare now..." William said, his hands and fingers intertwined as if in prayer.

"William, you are home! Don't you see yet? All this pain is your badge of honor. Your destiny is at hand. This is home, William. This pain will never leave you and you will never leave it," Milena said firmly, "It's all going to be all right, William, trust me. Now let's move on to our next destination, shall we?"

"No, please, I don't…" William tried to say. But Milena had already put her right hand on his left shoulder.

And that excruciating light came again…

Part 2 – June Moon

William found himself trapped somewhere dark where he couldn't move. He was still shaken by the loss of his alternate son and the massacre he had witnessed. He had never so been bewildered before, yet a new confusion shadowed the former one.

He was looking out of a pair of weirdly familiar eyes. A woman's hair swinging back and forth covered most of her features. It was hard to see the face long enough clearly with all that hair. But the eyes… He recognized them. The look in those eyes was pain pretending to be pleasure. He tried to look round but realized he couldn't move his head. Hell, he couldn't even see his body. All he could see was her head moving in some kind of rhythm.

"Welcome to your next lesson, William," Milena calmly said from somewhere he couldn't see. It sounded like welcoming an audience to a theater.

"Milena, where are you? I can't see you! Can't see myself, either. What's going on? Where are we?" asked a panicked William.

"Don't be a whiny baby again, William; keep your cool, it's all good, don't worry," Milena said. She sounded friendlier and nearer now, "This time, it's going to be a tad more claustrophobic I'm afraid. As we will be occupying someone else's head for a bit."

"Whose?" asked William, dreading the answer, the answer he thought he already knew.

"Rachel's! Or Olivia as she's called here. Yuppie!" she said with a wicked, hysterical laugh, "Nothing is more adorable than a lovers' reunion. I love it! It may be a wee bit wetter than a romantic one though, ha-ha-ha!"

"You cruel bitch! You enjoy this, don't you?" asked William, sickened.

"Hell yeah! Why not? You should too, William. This is once in a lifetime experience. You might as well enjoy it. After all, you know the saying: if rape is inevitable, lie down and enjoy it... Yummy!" Milena was smacking her lips.

"What now, you'll kill my wife too? To teach me a lesson in your twisted, fucked up way?"

"Me? Who have I killed so for? I'm just a guide, William. A tour guide of sights you cannot fathom other than by experiencing them. I don't kill. I show. And who said she'd die?"

"Spare me your fancy lectures. Let's get on with whatever the hell this is," he snapped.

"OK, OK, hold your horses. First, let's get you up to speed."

William felt a hand on his unseen head; a quick fainting sensation was followed by pain and pressure at his rear.

"God, it hurts, what's this?" William wailed.

"Oh, this? That's a six-inch ding-a-ling penetrating your wife's ass a hundred strokes a minute," Milena burst out laughing, "What a ride, right?"

William's eyes locked on Rachel's – or in this case, Olivia's – looking back at him from the mirror above the bed, kneeling on all fours, a fat pig behind her back panting, sweating and moaning.

The eyes, thought William, *They're not the eyes of my beautiful wife. They're not the bright eyes of the mother of my children.*

His thoughts were interrupted by a spasm inside him.

"Ye-ha! Here comes the champion!" yelled Milena.

The man's moans hurt his ears.

The fat pig got up, put on his pants, grabbed his clothes, and headed to the bathroom.

Olivia lay down on her back, looked at the ceiling, pulled the cheap quilt up to her neck, and waited in silence. A few minutes later, the man re-emerged, fully clothed. Olivia did not turn her head to look at him. He plodded towards the bed, threw something beside her and walked out without a word.

William found himself watching the small window through Olivia's eyes, a few feet from the bed. It was dark outside. Neon lights in various colors winked among the raindrops licking the window. Under it was an electric radiator, clearly a later addition. The window frame looked rotten. Red curtains flimsy as peeled skin flanked the window. Evidently not meant to block the sun – or anything else for that matter – but rather frame the stage of a shadow play. The room didn't look that high above street level. He could see the signs on other buildings – mostly bars and clubs. He felt the chill wind sweeping into the room from the cracks. The whole scene screamed *gutter*. All he could hear was pipes rattling in the corners and noises from the floor above.

A loud banging on the door cut through the silence like a sharp knife.

"Come on, bitch, get up and hit the streets. Time is money!" someone shouted from the other side.

"I'm coming…" Olivia replied in a trembling voice.

She got up. Grabbed the money from the bed and headed towards the bathroom. The dark green room consisted of a bed, a single nightstand without a lamp, a wooden chair where Rachel hung her pink, short leathery coat, and a vanity table with a small round mirror, cracked. That was it. The whole space couldn't be more than a hundred and fifty square feet.

This room is made for speed, not comfort, thought William.

Opening the creaky bathroom door, which nearly banged into the washbasin, she turned the water on and started to wash herself. Her hands looked much older and wrinkled than his Rachel's. That freezing water made his unseen body shiver. He could feel every last thing she did. He felt the goose pimples on Olivia's body.

As she lifted her head, wet her hair and combed it back, her entire face came into sight. Much thinner than her Rachel version, she had sharper cheekbones; most of her eyebrows seemed to be gone, replaced by a tattoo-like paint. It was neither black nor brown but a cheap purple. Her hair was lank; white roots indicated that it had been a few months since she'd last touched it up. She was covered in bruises, especially over her lower body. What William found most troubling, however, was the scar on her left cheek. It stretched from the ear to the chin. It was the same color as her skin, suggesting it must have happened over a year ago; it wouldn't have healed fully otherwise.

Who did it and why? he thought bitterly, *Who could have done this disgrace to my beautiful wife?*

"What happened to her? Is she a hooker now?" he asked.

"Yes, she is, William. And not a very classy one from the looks of the room, don't you agree? Not to mention the back door service, ha-ha-ha!" Milena replied in a teasing tone that he found infuriating.

"Stop laughing, you sadistic bitch!" he shouted at the unseen Milena, wishing he could see her so he could spit at her lovely face.

"Hey, take it easy! I'm not the bad guy here, remember. None of this is my fault. As for my teasing, screw you! I can do whatever I want. Remember what I said on the bench beside the lake? I'm not here to comfort you. I told you I would ride you like a bull from the get-go. So shut the fuck up and focus," Milena raged back.

"Focus on what? What's the point of all this? What happened here? Where am I in this story?"

"This is no story, William. Just another reality that could have been. As for where you are, I'm sorry to inform you that you are dead, Pups."

"Dead?… How?" asked William.

"We will come to that."

"Stop with all the mystery and tell it all for God's sake."

"All right, cool your jets. Here's the whole story in a snapshot: In here, you are Lucas Jameson. You were born in Kansas into a modest farmer family. You lived near a charming town called Fort Stone. It was a bit like the Smallville of the Kent family. You had a wonderful childhood among corn and cattle with your three brothers. You were the oldest. Your father sold what he grew and invested the money back into his livelihood. Your mother cooked, took care of you four monsters and your father. It was more than enough for all of you to live a happy and decent life," Milena said. She paused for a sigh and continued:

"You've known Olivia since childhood. You know how everyone knows everybody in small towns. You opened up to her when you were both fifteen. It took many sessions of encouragement from your friends. You liked her so much that you were really scared she would reject you. In fact, she liked you too but you know how girls are, they are good at keeping their reactions in check, as she did. But inside, she waited impatiently for you to ask her out. What stupid games you humans play!" With a sarcastic laugh, she carried on. "One day, after school, you asked her if you could give her a lift in your truck, which you had borrowed from your father for that purpose alone. You had never driven it before that day and had little experience, so you nearly busted the clutch on the way and almost ran over a squirrel. She found your anxiety sweet. When you got there, you were on the verge of backing out but at the last minute, you found your nerve and asked her out. She said yes with a cute smile, walked out and started walking to the front door. You stared all the way. You thought she was the most beautiful creature you had ever seen: *She is like an exquisite gazelle*. Just when she was about to open the door, she turned her head, her hair flicking, and gave you a smile. You never forgot that look. Your first date was on a Saturday. You took her to dinner and a movie afterward. Typical Kansas-style date. You spent your whole allowance on the town's most fancy restaurant. At the end of that night, you kissed her for the first time. That kiss sealed both your fates. After that, you were inseparable. Most high school sweethearts are motivated by teenage sex in the rear of their trucks. You were not. You loved each other dearly. You made plans for your future together. Where you want to live, what you will do, how many children you will have. You even decided their names. Liam if it's a boy, Violet if it's a girl. It was like living in a Disney movie, fairies and all." He could almost hear Milena's smile, a wry smile. One that's the precursor of something bitter. She paused again. For a moment, William was worried she was gone. He was relieved when she resumed speaking.

"But this was no movie. It was real life. Trouble started when a global agriculture and livestock company opened offices in town. They were so big that lowering prices even at the risk of losing money was of no consequence for them. They lowered the prices so much that your father could only sell half his cattle that year. They squeezed the little guys into a corner and then bought them out one by one, at much lower prices than even the bare cost of the animals. Your father resisted for a year; in the end, though, he had no choice but to sell all his cattle to them. All he had left was corn. It was either less money or no money at all," Milena's soft and steady voice reminded William of his nanny's bedtime stories, in his original life. Only this was a much darker one.

"Your father held his head high. He was a proud man. He did his best to keep up your standards. But there was more trouble ahead. A year after the cattle, he was having trouble selling the corn too. *They* did it again. Same story, different product. He tried to hold his own, he even offered them an exclusive deal. But they wanted to *own*, not to live and let live. In the end, he had to sell it all, the fields, the barns, even the house your grandfather had built with his bare hands. He begged *them* to keep the house at least, but they said they wouldn't buy any of it without the house; they needed a facility for their management team. You were about to apply for college then. It was not meant to be. What your father was left with wasn't enough to sending all four boys to college. You made no fuss; you knew it wouldn't be fair to your brothers. Your father found a house to rent downtown. He would have bought one, but all the money from the sale had gone to cover the bank loans. Your mother started work at the local diner, cooking her wonderful dishes. You, unable to go to college, started as a handyman after you graduated. You needed the money to marry Olivia and get your own place. For a while, things looked on the up. Olivia fell pregnant with Liam a few months after the wedding. A new life would breathe happiness and hope into your family, you hoped. Your father wasn't doing that well though. Too old to find a well-paid job or start over, he became depressed and took to drink. Not violent in any way, just losing it every passing day. There were weeks he barely left the house. He was just sitting there, staring blankly into the old TV set for hours.

"One day, your mother came home, walked into the bedroom to check on him and found him hanging by his neck from the crystal chandelier they'd been given as a wedding present twenty-five years earlier. You were twenty-one. She called you to take him down before your brothers got back from school - the police said they were busy and wouldn't be back for another three hours. So she had to call you. He was too heavy for her to do it on her own. Looking at his face, white as a sheet, and his dry tongue lolling out on the left corner of his mouth, you remembered all those times playing the lick the cheek game with him. How strong and invincible he'd seemed then. You burst into tears but quickly got a hold of yourself. It was the worst day of your life; at least you thought so at the time."

Milena paused for a second. The last sentence and her second sigh warned William of worse things to come. Her unseen hand touched his head tenderly, a tenderness she had said she would not show again just before their first cosmic trip, in that pitch-black emptiness with him lying on her sweet lap.

She continued as William listened in silence.

"Your father's suicide was devastating for you all. Your mother aged suddenly, your brothers started running with the wrong crowd and regularly got into trouble with the law. Your income wasn't stable, and taking care of your wife and three-year-old child got harder and harder. But you were not your father. You were stronger, younger and more ambitious. You made the most rational decision anyone in your situation could do. You joined the army. You'd be away for some time but you would have a stable income to send to your family; and serving your country was one of the most honorable things you could think of. Olivia was supportive; she was proud. But she wasn't thrilled by the idea of you leaving for many months. One day, it did come to pass: you were sent to Afghanistan. You were twenty-three at the time."

"Did I die there? Is that what happened? Is that what caused my wife to fall into this life?" asked William.

"Yes, it was there you died," Milena replied, "But it was not a soldier's death. Neither was it the cause of your wife's despair. It's a little more complicated than that, William."

"Go on, I'm listening," said William. They were not in the room any longer: he saw empty streets and sidewalks, he saw Olivia's cheap red high heels, he saw the hungry eyes of men lurking in the shadows, salivating as they ogled her.

God, how the hell did it come to this? How did my lovely wife turn into this cheap bit of flesh? he thought, depressed.

"Your time in Afghanistan started fine. You made friends there; it made you feel whole again. Something you'd lost after your father's death. But then conflicts flared up in the region. Not a day went by that you didn't get into an armed clash with the resistance. One day, during an operation in a town full of civilians, you witnessed things. Things your honorable soldier mind couldn't accept. Things you'd never have expected from your brothers-in-arms," Milena said.

"What kind of things?"

"I'm sorry to do this again, William. But somethings cannot be told; they have to be seen," she said. William understood what she was about to do.

"I'm ready. Let's get on with it." Olivia was now leaning against a wall, one leg bent. *What a cliché*, he thought.

He closed his eyes and waited for the inevitable. The last thing he saw before the crescendo was the red neon lights above the club door across the road: *Boiler Room*.

And then came the bang, just like in their previous journey, but much harder.

His mind filled with images and sensations like a million bees stinging him at the same time. The noise of explosions, gunfire, aircraft overhead and smell of burned flesh. It was like nothing he had ever experienced or even had thought could possibly endure.

"Go, go, go, go!" barked Sergeant Brick, a big bruiser born into three generations of soldiers, ordering them to enter the premises. A small mud house with no windows. It was a tight fit for half a dozen armed men.

"Secure the perimeter, no one gets out!" he ordered the privates standing outside.

"Perimeter secured, Sarge! Get down to the floor, get down, now!" Corporal Alex shouted to those inside. A fierce hulk nicknamed T-Rex due to his enormous mouth, tiny teeth and relatively short arms for that strapping body.

There were three men, two women and four children inside. It looked too small for them all: they had to be living practically on top of one another.

The household sank down to their knees.

"Don't you fucking move, you camel bangers!" yelled Private Morton, a weasel who'd do anything T-Rex told him to.

"I don't like the look on their faces, Sarge; I don't like it, they're about to try something, I'm telling you..." said an agitated T-Rex.

"Keep 'em covered, Corporal, cool it..." replied Brick, "Morton: frisk them!"

At Morton's nervous approach, one of the men reached his left hand inside his jacket.

"He's gonna shoot, he's gonna shoot!" T-Rex yelled and aimed his rifle. The man, who looked like he was about to draw a gun from inside his jacket, was saying something; but the words were lost in all that shouting.

T-Rex pulled the trigger and peppered the man with bullets. The other men on their knees screamed, trying to get up.

"Fire, fire!" shouted Sergeant Brick. Only he and T-Rex did the shooting. Morton froze while Lucas stood guard outside. The two men who were trying to get up fell down, never to rise again.

"You stupid fucks!" T-Rex spat on the dead men.

Only the women and the children were alive now. Looking in, Lucas felt sick at the sight of the frightened children. The eyes... with unsuspecting, unfiltered, pure and absolute fear. *What if they were little Liam's eyes*, he thought.

"Sarge, better take a look at this..." Morton said, picking up something like a business card from the floor.

"Give it here," said Sergeant Brick. The guns were still pointing at the women and children. He raised the card to his eyes.

Army Pass
Press

"Fuck, fuck!" Sergeant Brick bellowed, "Fucking fool! He should've said!"

"What is it, Sarge?" asked T-Rex.

"He was one of ours; he was Press. Shit!" Sergeant Brick sounded regretful.

"Holy shit, this is bad, Sarge, this is bad..." Morton said.

"What do we do now, Sarge?" T-Rex yelled.

"I don't know, I don't know. No one told us there were Press in the field. God damn it!"

Taking another look at the dead man's face, Sergeant Brick said, "Wait a minute. I know this guy! I knew I knew him! I saw him a month ago at HQ... Oh, shit, this guy is not Press, he is from Bethasta."

"Bethasta? The arms manufacturer Bethasta?" Morton asked in a panic.

"*That* Bethasta. This is bad, this is bad in every way," Sergeant Brick said, "Everyone, turn off your body cams, now!"

"But Sarge, there'll be a gap and we've already been transmitting," said T-Rex.

"Shut up and do as I say," snapped Sergeant Brick.

Everyone obeyed, except for Lucas.

"Private, turn it off now, this is an order!"

"But Sarge, it's against protocol," Lucas protested.

Sergeant Brick stomped over and turned off Lucas' camera. "I don't think you get the gravity of the situation, Private. We just killed the representative of an American arms dealer in an enemy cell. Are you aware of the implications? We'll be the scapegoats for this mess. We'll be accused of engineering this shit. You think we can keep it secret? You think the big guns will take responsibility? We'll all be fucked."

"Sarge, what do we do now?" asked T-Rex.

"We finish it. It can't get out."

"What do you mean finish, Sarge?" asked T-Rex.

"I mean no survivors, Corporal!"

At these words, Lucas left his post and stormed in.

"Sarge, what's going on? Let's get out of here; our mission is done. It's nobody's fault, he reached into his jacket, anyone would have thought he was hostile. That's not our problem; we're not the ones responsible for this shit show," he pleaded.

"No, this would ruin all our lives. We can't let this come to light. We'll be court-martialed. They'll pin this on us, do you understand me? You think anyone high up will own up to knowing anything about this? We'll get the fall. This is big!" Sergeant Brick said worried, looking down.

"Sarge, please, let's get out of here, I'll stand up for you, I know what happened, they'll see it wasn't your fault," said Lucas.

"It's easy for you to say, you're not the one who pulled the trigger," T-Rex intervened.

"He's right. We need to finish this once and for all. Do you hear me, Private, this in an order!" Sergeant Brick barked at Lucas.

"No, no, I won't take any part in this. And I won't let you do it either!" Lucas yelled as he saw Morton stomping towards him. The next thing he felt was the butt of Morton's gun slamming into his head. He fell down semi-conscious and saw the terror on the children's faces. It was like their own hopes were also down.

Lucas barely managed a "No, please…"

As the women shielded the children, one of the children, a small boy around five, broke into a loud cry. The others joined in the screaming; all that noise meant something was wrong.

"They're just kids, Sarge, they don't understand what's happened here. They can't say anything. They don't even know English," Morton said, hoping to get out of this mess.

"We can't risk it; what if they know everything," T-Rex said.

"He's right. We can't risk it," Sergeant Brick approved, "We're in this together, soldier."

T-Rex and Morton nodded reluctantly. T-Rex slapped his own face a couple of times and yelled a war cry. Morton mouthed a rueful "Fuck!"

Lucas tried to get up and stop them. But he couldn't. That blow to the head had temporarily disabled his motor functions.

And then he heard his sergeant:

"God, forgive me…"

"No, Sarge, no!" Lucas screamed, still lying on the packed earth. The other three aimed at the children and women. A loud scream filled the windowless room.

The multiple automatic shots only lasted a few seconds.

Hot blood splashed Lucas's face as screams died down.

"No! What have you done?! They were just kids! Oh, God, you murdered them!"

"Shut up, Jameson, just shut the fuck up! We just killed their fathers, their kin. What do you think they'd grow up to be, huh? They'd have dreamt of revenge from today on until they were old enough to take up arms. They were animals, anyway," Sergeant Brick shouted back. His mind had already justified his action.

"T-Rex: tell me what happened," Sergeant Brick asked T-Rex.

"We entered the premises as a unit, Sarge, including Private Jameson. The hostiles reached for their guns and started to shoot at us," T-Rex replied.

As T-Rex recited the script, he grabbed one of the dead 'hostile's' guns from the outside, brought it in and fired six shots at the wall behind them, "With God's grace, none of us were wounded, Sir!" He then placed the gun in one of the dead men's hands.

"Good. And Private Morton? What is your recollection of the incident?"

"Same, Sarge!" Morton confirmed.

"What about you, Private Jameson?" asked Sergeant Brick, handgun pointing at Lucas, "Do you have anything to add?"

"You're not gonna get away with it, I swear to God, I won't let you off the hook!"

"Yeah, we'll see about that," said Sergeant Brick, "Burn this place down, just in case," he ordered T-Rex and Morton. And then whacked Lucas on the back of the head.

The next thing Lucas saw was the white ceiling of the squadron infirmary.

"I remember it all," William said to Milena, "They killed babies, oh God..." he moaned. Lucas' memories rushing into his mind once again hurt like hell.

"Yes, they did. This is what war is. Not a glorious thing to celebrate with holidays every year but children's screams and the slaughter of babies. It is one of the best ways to earn money for them. Start a war, stoke it, sell weapons to both sides, keep it going as long as you can. It's always been that way. Do you remember what happened afterward?"

Olivia was arguing with a skinny bum now. A drunkard, by the looks of it, out of a shitty alley, waving a couple of banknotes at her face. William's head felt too crowded to hear what they were saying.

"I reported the incident to our CO. Gave him the full story. I protested, even threatened to go to the Press if they were not court-marshaled. I told him about the bodycams," William replied, "He seemed shocked and repelled by it. Assured me they'd be dealt with in due course but I had to carry on, for the time being; we were in the middle of an operation."

William's head was about to explode. He paused for a second. There was something else the CO had said, which he hadn't given much thought to at the time but made sense now.

"He also asked me if I'd spoken to anyone else about it. I said no, even though I'd told it all to Olivia on the phone. He told me to keep this between us for the time being and he would deal with them as soon as the next operation was complete."

"And?" Milena asked in the confident tone of someone who already knew the answer.

"And then... I died," whispered William, "The last thing I remember was the gunfight outside a rebel town. I had asked for a transfer to another unit the previous day. But everything happened so fast. There was another mission the next day. I hadn't slept at all that night. I remember my team giving me funny looks. I was scared to close my eyes even for a minute. God, it hurts again, everything is piling up on one another. Louis, Gabriel, my other life in Kansas, Olivia, my father, the brothers I never met!"

He would have sunk to the floor for a few minutes but he wasn't even there; he had no body.

"It's all right, William, take your time..." he heard Milena's voice.

Pausing to catch his breath, he continued:

"I felt edgy in the morning. All my instincts said something bad was going to happen. I was a soldier, though; I had no choice but to ignore that sense of foreboding. Oh, shit, it's all coming back now," he said in pain, "Once we were on the ground, all hell broke loose. I mean really loose. We were under heavy artillery fire. The rebels were trying to seize back a town we took a few months ago. We were there to circle them from the outside and support the troops inside the town. I remember Sergeant Brick shouting at me. Pushing me forward before the others. He said they were covering me. And just when I raced onward, I felt a sharp sting in the back of my head. After that, it's all blank... It was them who shot me, weren't they?"

"Unfortunately, yes, they were the ones, William. I'm sorry. This is how you died. Betrayed by the men you called brothers. It is up to me to tell you what happened afterward," said Milena, taking the reins up again. "Your suspicious death right after what you told Olivia was more than enough for her to go to the Press. Her grief over her lifelong sweetheart's death was second only to her frustration. She was ruined, totally devastated but she was mad! She knew you weren't killed in action. She knew it in her bones. She went to all the mainstream media but most of them didn't give two fucks. Those who did quickly dropped the story when the incident was denied by the military and Bethasta. It was like nothing ever happened; like you never died. Nobody cared. Only after her persistent inquires and constant social media posts that a local independent internet news agency covered your story, which led to a bigger, national one picking it up from there. That's when all the craziness began," Milena said.

"How?"

"Well, the story went viral on social media. That's when *they* started to get nervous. And when they get nervous, their first instinct is to attack. Oh and how they attacked! First, they dug up everything they could about you and your whole family. How your father went bankrupt and had to sell his business and estate, which he blamed on one of the biggest companies that contribute to their economy. There were allegations about how unpatriotic he was, what an enemy of the state he was for blocking the development of capitalism, how he tried to cheat the bank by cooking his company books."

"No way would anyone believe this shit!" said William.

"You'd be surprised what people are ready to believe, as long as it is incriminating. No one wants to hear how good or successful someone is. No one is proud of another who does better than them. They get envious. They congratulate in whispers but accuse in scowls. That's the way it is with you. That's how you've been indoctrinated to act. So yes, they believed every word of it. They wanted to believe so they can pretend that their most sacred institutions are exactly as advertised. Honorable, righteous and glorious," said Milena.

"This is absurd. Everyone who knew my father could testify to his decency."

"Only a few did. But their statements were never published. Most of them just pretended to be shocked. "He hadn't been in his right mind for some time…" said an old neighbor. It was Olivia's turn next. To discredit her.

This time, the target was more suitable for their favorite smear campaign method: the one and only below the waist tactic. Oh, what a slut she was in high school, how she was trying to slander valiant soldiers and the army to extort money from the government. Their capacity for trashing knew no boundaries. Then the mainstream media declared her a traitor to her country. Even suggested she could be a Russian collaborator."

"What? No, no, this is beyond ridiculous; I'm speechless. A Russian collaborator? She was born and bred in a small Kansas town; how and why would she have been in league with another country working against her own?" asked William in shock.

"It doesn't matter. Once the genie was out of the box, there was no way to contain it anymore. Why do you think they always try their best to keep people ignorant, careless and hateful? It's all for such times. It's all to easily deceive them, no matter how preposterous the allegations. And this had all the right elements for a good night's entertainment: sex, betrayal, blackmail… People leaped at it! They wanted to chew it to the bone, suck it until there was no more juice left, revel in someone else's downfall and then, when it's all said and done, throw it out and wait the next one. Repeat it enough times and people will believe anything. Your own townsfolk, your neighbors, people who knew you and Oliva your whole lives crossed the road when they saw her on the sidewalk. Her boss at the local diner where your mother used to work fired her over a stupid excuse. Liam was bullied at school. Everyone found a reason to justify to crucify Olivia. Your brothers, who had left for God knows where about a year earlier, were nowhere to be found. And your mother was too sick to defend her. Her abusive piece of shit father was too busy drinking his life away in a nearby town. She was all alone. When her front door was daubed with pig blood, she had enough. A couple of days later, she packed up, grabbed Liam and headed to the big city, to make a new life. She cried her heart out all the way. Leaving her own town was too much to take. She stayed with an old friend for about a week. Looked for a good job but the country was in the clutches of a slump. Remember the banks, which were too big to fail, that were bailed out with your tax money? Another clutch of the big cabal machine. Another important member of *them*. So the self-serving hypocrisy of the government and the corrupt military, legitimized by the mainstream media and the finishing touch by the greedy bankers created the perfect storm that turned her life upside down. The only place that gave her a job was a bar in the inner bowels of the city. She took it without thinking, rented a one-room condo in the projects and started her new life the same night. For a few weeks, it went rather well. But as life got harder and costlier, she had to expand her job description. Taking care of Liam, paying her neighbors for babysitting, food, rent, it all piled up. Bartending for those low lives turned into being a hostess, which led to meeting the wrong kind of guy, which gave way to drug abuse, which meant needing more money, and voilà! You got yourself the new Olivia, the back door pleasurer junkie."

"Stop calling her that!" said William.

"Why? It's what she is now. It's just a statement of truth. This is the problem with you people. You're offended too easily, even by the truth. It's your fucking ego, your illusion of your self-importance, when in truth, you are nothing to the universe but what a worm is to you: irrelevant…"

"It's got nothing to do with my ego. This is my wife you're talking about," said William, finally in possession of every single memory of Olivia, which gave him the right to call her wife. It came naturally now.

"So what? Being your wife makes her a saint? She is human. Flesh, bones and hormones with fragile emotions, deep complexes and unrealistic dreams. Just like you. Just like every one of you. No better, no worse. This holier-than-thou attitude is your undoing and their gift. This is how they easily control you. Let me give you an example: when someone says, 'All humans are crooks,' no one stands up to protest. Hell, some may even call this remark progressive and on point. But when someone comes up and says, 'You're a crook, William,' you're offended and react much more harshly. Now this is ego. Individual interest and honor over the collective. When you're all called crooks, no one cares, no one is offended. When just one of you is called out, it's clobbering time. And they love it!"

"I don't care. Just don't call her that," said William.

"Well, I do care, William. You must not fall victim to their tricks. You must understand and know that individualism is their mantra for controlling you. Individualism through personal beauty, personal benefit, personal wealth, personal property, self-improvement, honor, and the most powerful of all, your ego. If they can grab you one by one, they can break you easily. If you are bonded together, you will be unbreakable," she said and continued, "Take a single branch, and you can snap it with no effort at all. If you grab ten branches bonded together, you can barely bend it. This is the power of the collective. This is one of the lessons you must learn from this journey."

"OK, consider me taught. Now what? Should I stay here and witness this misery?"

"Witness? You got it all wrong, William. You're to witness nothing. You're here to live through it," Milena said. William felt her hand on his head once more. *How cold*, he thought just before all that Olivia had to suffer plummeted onto his mind and detonated.

The pounding of her heart on seeing the grim-looking officer in his ceremonial uniform at her doorstep. The almost audible crack in her heart on hearing the news of her husband's death. The stinging in her eyes from crying endlessly in bed, curled up in the fetal position. The stuttering of her words when she had to explain to Liam that his father wouldn't be coming home again. The loneliness of her struggle in seeking justice. All the sweat pouring out of her on those nights full of nightmares, the lack of comfort, the cold on her skin, the sickness in her stomach from her friends' judgmental eyes, the desperation, the backache of working till the morning, the deliverance of the first injection of heroin and the despair that came when it wore out, the cries when social services took her son from her when she passed out high and set the living room on fire with a cigarette... The revolting stink of genitals and pubic hairs sticking to her tongue, gagging from those pigs shoving their dicks in her mouth, the unwillingness to live, the longing for the deliverance of death... All the pain, all the senses, all the anguish, uploaded onto William's mind at once.

"Nooo, ooh, nooo... It's too much, I can't take it, stop it, take it back!" he exclaimed.

"Feel it, William, embrace it; it's yours forever, it won't go away. This is what millions of people get from this world! Know it, remember it! This is your deliverance; this is your enlightenment!" Milena snapped.

Just when he thought he'd rather die than live this nightmare, a powerful euphoria flashed over his unseen body. Opening his eyes a crack, he saw a needle on the arm he was looking at.

"No, Liv, don't do it, please honey, I love you..." he tried to shout but didn't have the strength... So he just wept, for someone he never actually met, except in his mind.

A thin trickle of blood emanated from the point where the needle had pierced the skin; it ran down the arm of its own accord, pooling in and overflowing track marks.

That euphoria gave way to a blurry sight of rain and a cloudy sky with a partial view of the moon. They both remembered the time when they were sixteen, lying side by side on the green fields by Lucas's farmhouse on a clear June night, watching the moon, holding hands, dreaming about the future and making love till the sun came up.

Then the light faded and darkness spread just before the agonizing flash banged again.

Part 3 - Dr. Climbhobble

The first thing William heard when he opened his eyes was the waves and the splashing of water on his face. He could taste salt. He barely found the strength to lift his head from the damp wood. Milena had clearly set up a new nightmare to torture him; what else could feel so depressing? At long last sitting up, he looked around. He was in a slightly larger size rowboat. Apparently adrift in the middle of the sea, with no land visible anywhere. It seemed like the golden hour but he couldn't figure out if the sun was rising or setting; he had no sense of direction or time. The wind was so stiff that he nearly lost his balance and fell overboard. Bending down, he grabbed the oarlock.

"Milena? Where are you?" he hollered. No one answered. He was about to yell for Milena a second time when a faint groan came from the aft – which was covered by a large cloth.

There must be someone underneath it, he thought.

He looked around for Milena once again, hoping his guide would explain what the hell was going on this time.

Funny, he thought, *how someone you blamed and despised for torturing you was the one you sought out in times of desperation. You fucking hypocrite.* But this was no time for self-criticism; someone was underneath that cloth and he was alone with them in the middle of a raging sea.

Maybe Milena placed some monsters from hell there; now that *would be a good end*, he thought with a grim, sickly smile, *or maybe it is my father. Even those monsters would bow down and kiss his ring.*

You know you have to do it, William... You have to go over and lift that stained cloth peppered with holes and see who or what is under it. There's no escape from it. Milena's sick game's rules clearly demand it, he said to himself.

God damn you, you beautiful, cruel monster... God damn you to hell.

William took a deep breath, held it for a few seconds and exhaled as slowly as he could. It made him dizzy, dulled his fears long enough to move and grab the dangling corner of the cloth. With another deep breath, he tugged it off without exhaling.

He gasped aloud in shock.

"Oh my God, my babies, my babies..." he wailed, "Rachel, my love, my babies... "

Consternation and horror showed on exhausted faces of his wife and children. It was like they didn't understand him.

"Ahmed! -------" exclaimed the woman and said something... William didn't understand the words after "Ahmed". She was speaking in another language. Some language that sounded Middle Eastern.

"Rachel, it's me my love, William, your husband," he said as she looked at him bewildered, "Answer me, Rachel, it's me, William."

"Ahmed, ---------" she said again in a tongue he couldn't understand. She looked more surprised than pleased.

William took a step back. He was dying to hug his wife and children but there was something wrong. Giving up on trying to communicate, he stared into their faces. There was something different. Not just the clothes but something different in their looks too. Their skins were darker. His Rachel's emerald eyes were now dark brown. His pretty Candice's blonde hair was reddish-brown. Their features were quite similar, with slight differences. Eyebrows, lips, eyelashes: they all looked Middle Eastern. He examined every little detail astonished when everything juddered into a stop.

The waves, the sounds, the boat's movement, the sharp breaths of his family; it all froze in time. That's when his eyes caught the only movement that still existed to his rear: thick, long crimson tresses gently undulating in a wind from an unknown direction.

"Welcome to your third trip, William. I'm sorry to have joined it late but it was by design," Milena said, looking at the horizon where the sun was either rising or setting. Her back was turned to William, "This one, I'm afraid, will be far more demanding than the previous ones."

"Milena, where are we? Why is my family different?" asked William.

"You're in the middle of the Mediterranean Sea, William, trying to reach Greece. You're running away from the war in Syria."

"Oh, God, not another one. What's the matter with you? Why can't you let me go? I've seen enough," William moaned.

"I'm sorry but not yet, William."

"Yes, you careless son of a bitch, not yet!" someone said behind him.

Startled by the voice, William swung round in a reflex. What – or more accurately, whom – he saw was petrifying.

"Did you really think you could get off this easy?" asked the man.

William was flabbergasted; he gulped wordlessly.

"Cat got your tongue?"

The man was William's spitting image. As he gaped at himself, Milena explained:

"You are refugees, William. Your name, as you may have already guessed, is Ahmed. Your wife is Fairuz, your son is Yousef, your daughter is Malika. Syrians born and bred for more than six generations."

"Nice to meet you, William. You seem dismayed. Good. You better be," the man said somewhat crossly, "But I need you to be sharp. So let me introduce myself: I am Ahmed. The man you could have been in another life."

Still unable to find the right words, William chose to stare stupidly.

"This is our family, William. Just one of the thousands of families you ignore every day," Ahmed said. He had a rough accent, "You must wonder how the hell we ended up here, right?

"I'm sorry. I truly am," William spoke at last. Without knowing what he'd hear next.

"Yeah, me too. But I'm not interested in your pity," Ahmed said, "I need your focus William; so shut up and listen to the story. And wipe that fake sympathy off your face."

William tried to do what he said but he wasn't sure what to feel at that moment.

"While you were peacefully sleeping in your warm beds, we were fighting for our lives," Ahmed began, "We lived quietly, in peace in a country constantly in turmoil. Our family was in deliveries for dozens of years. It was our father who started as a porter when he was just thirteen. It was him who, with his vision and hard work, invested everything he earned in our first truck. It was a small one.

A secondhand piece of junk but to him, it was glorious. This was the milestone for our family's security and good life. When he left us the business, we had more than a hundred latest model trucks. He had high hopes for us. He raised us as well as he could possibly do. He taught us the importance of decency, honesty, mercy, the value of hard work over making a quick buck."

"Wait a minute, what do you mean *us*? This is not my life: it's yours; nothing to do with me! Why the hell are you talking to me like I was responsible for whatever happened to *you*?" asked William.

"Oh, you are wrong, my friend. This was your life as much as mine. You and I are bonded, whether you accept it or not!" Ahmed said calmly, "I guess I need to do better, then."

His rough hands landed on William's head.

"No, please, not again…" begged William. But it was too late. Memories filled his already crowded mind and started to collapse on top of the previous ones. He cried out in pain.

"Yes, swallow it all," Ahmed said, "You see now, don't you? Tell me, tell me all!"

Now in agony, William had sunk to his knees. He experienced everything Ahmed had lived, compressed into a single touch.

"Leave me alone!" he shouted, tormented.

"No, you can't get rid of me easily," Ahmed replied, "Tell me, what did he teach us? Start talking now, you piece of shit!"

"He told us that life is not always rainbows and butterflies, instead, life is a continuous and never-ending struggle. Real happiness, he said, is hidden in this struggle, all right?" William started to speak reluctantly.

"Material satisfaction always leads to another material need and it goes on and on, till you turn into a

119

serpent swallowing its own tail forever and ever," Ahmed continued William's sentence in their father's voice.

"But real happiness lies in the joy of the struggle. In the hardships that forge you like a masterpiece of steel. You need to give in to the struggle, so that you may flourish. But give into the worldly property and bodily desires, then this world will devour you piece by piece, until you are nothing but an empty shell. Useless, worthless and soon enough lifeless," William continued.

Moaning, he stopped as the rest of this memory rushed through his mind.

"You need to feed your soul with science, arts, music, philosophy... All that befits men's splendor," Ahmed finished the words.

"Exactly what my grandfather told me..." William said, surprised.

It was Milena who replied this time: "I know."

William carried on:

"When our father died, we didn't feel lost, like most sons of great men do. Because we were ready to become our own men, take care of our family, our business and take the reins of our own life. And we didn't disappoint. In our leadership, the business grew, our family prospered in every way, financially and morally. We were simply happy..."

Ahmed's memories brought back William's own, of the death of his own father Daniel. He had also been simply happy afterward but not in the same way as Ahmed. He remembered accepting condolences at the funeral.

"I'm very sorry for your loss, William; your father was an extraordinary man," the mayor had said as William stood by the open casket.

"Thank you very much, Mr. Mayor, I appreciate it," he had replied. His real self's answer was very different though.

He was the greatest asshole that has ever walked this earth; you know it, I know it. He was extraordinarily generous with his bribes though, right? You two-faced vulture, his inner voice had said and spat at the Mayor's face.

"Someone like Daniel Rudned comes once in a lifetime. You have very big shoes to fill William but I'm sure you are up to the task; he had great expectations of you," the chairman of their biggest rival had said.

"Thank you, Mr. Turpman, I will do my best," he had replied. Again, his alter-ego had interrupted.

Yeah, he was one of a kind for sure. A unique son of a bitch enough for ten lifetimes. You must have planned a celebration tonight, right? Now that the idiot son got his hands on the wheel; you can finally realize your dreams: destroying us.

Accepting condolences from everyone who was someone, he had turned to look at his father's casket from time to time, feigning sadness, and wondering if any of those hypocrites could tell. What if they did? They themselves were masters of that art, anyway, much more accomplished in deception than he could ever be. As he had gazed at his father's face, he had marveled at the skill of the undertaker's make-up artist for putting a smile on that stern face and thought *Wow, they really deserve every penny!*

His first encounter with death was when he was only eight. His aunt – his father's older sister – had been diagnosed with bone cancer and died just in six weeks. His mother had been the one to break the news, quite nervously, William recalled. She was afraid to explain the concept of death to a mere child. As she had explained how death was a natural part of life and everyone would eventually die, all William thought of was why he wasn't sad. How could he have been so indifferent to the untimely death of a close relation? He had felt terribly guilty. Felt the need to cry somehow. Forced himself to shed a few tears. He had found it difficult to weep for his aunt. Then he had thought about his father. Resentment had followed instantly. Only then had he been able to cry freely. Those tears were not of sorrow but of wrath.

He had been forcing himself similarly at his father's funeral but it was no use. This time, his happiness had overcome his fury. A grown man shouldn't cry in front of people anyway; so he had put on his silent, strong mask. Appearances were the most important thing.

I'm glad you're dead, he had said in his mind, silent laughter accompanying him every time he looked at that casket. All the same, guilt did visit him in bed that night. As if he had no right to be happy whether his father was alive or dead. There was no way out for him. Even when he was free of that monster's shackles, he was still a prisoner.

Ahmed's voice interrupted those thoughts.

"What happened next?"

"Then the civil war began…" replied William.

"That's right; and how did we react?"

"We ignored it and carried on with our lives as it was nothing. We thought with all our wealth, the war would never touch us, we'd have been protected, that it was just a revolt in the slums, it would have been crushed as quick as it had started," William replied. He felt like he was in an oral exam he hadn't revised for.

"Yes, we certainly thought so, didn't we?"

"But we were rich, why didn't we leave sooner for another country, before the clash escalated, while we still had our wealth?" asked William, "I can't remember the rest."

It wasn't true, though. It was coming to him but he was afraid to face it all. He tried to block the memories at the gates. He pushed as hard as he could.

"Oh, no, you don't," Ahmed said, "Stop it or I will do it for you."

"Please, I can't take it. My mind is about to crash," William pleaded. But Ahmed was unrelenting.

Yelling, "Get on with it!" he kicked William in the chest, toppling him backward.

William groaned as the memories stormed in now that his concentration was disturbed.

"Oh, fuck!"

"Yes, fuck is right," Ahmed said, "Now carry on, asshole."

William pulled himself together and got up, groaning in incredible agony, gripping his head, as though trying to hold the last bit of his remaining sanity with his bare hands before it flew away forever.

"We didn't leave, because we were too proud to do so. We struggled till the end. Just like our father taught us. Fairuz begged us to leave but we didn't listen. When the resistance soldiers asked for support money, we refused. They offered to buy our trucks, less than what they were worth, of course. We refused that too. They warned us that this was a good chance for us, that everything was going to get worse and we should take this opportunity to leave while we still could. They said they had no problem with us, as they knew we were never into politics and were different from the other elites who sided with the government to protect their own interests. It wasn't that we weren't sympathetic to their cause, it was because of the way they asked – or should I say – demanded. We weren't people who would be bullied; so we resisted. And they were right. It got much worse in a matter of weeks. Nobody knew who was who or what their agenda was. There was all kinds of organizations, terrorist groups, intelligence agencies, opportunists, sycophants everywhere. Each one worse than the other. Fairuz begged us again and again to sell the company, take everything we could carry and leave the country. But we refused. The struggle would bring us victory and salvation, just like our father said."

"But it didn't," Ahmed said.

"But it didn't," William repeated, "Once the war got chaotic enough, our business and trucks were pillaged by the same guys that had offered to buy them earlier. No one protected us. They were so cross with us, they even invaded our home, ransacked it, took everything they found and threw us out. We had to stay with one of our employees for a month before we found some money from an old friend to buy our way out of the country. But that money could only afford this shitty boat and two oars after paying the guys who arranged it all, bribing customs officials, a coast guard officer, buying some food and clothing for the trip. The compass we bought with our last money from the street dealer, which he claimed is what the pros are using, turned out to be a fake."

"That's why we are drifting aimlessly wherever the waves take us," Ahmet continued, "You may as well throw it overboard. It's in your pocket."

William checked his coat's pockets; the compass was in the right one. It was much lighter than it should have been.

How come this guy couldn't figure it out, he wondered, referring to his doppelgänger Ahmed. But he also remembered buying the compass and his unsuspecting naïveté.

"Because you were distracted," Milena spoke this time.

That's when William realized that she had been able to read his mind all along.

"So you have known what I was thinking all along, then?" asked William. It was strange that he wasn't shocked; all the same, he felt desecrated. Then a sense of peace came upon him. The kind of peace when you accept your fate and stop fighting.

"We're all going to die here, aren't we?" he asked Milena.

"Yes, I'm afraid you will. This is part of the process. But two things will happen before you do," Milena revealed, "First, you will understand what caused the situation you and your family are in. You will see that in the world we live, some fights cannot be won. It doesn't matter whether you are decent, honest or wise. Because the game is rigged to a point where only the house wins. That was your mistake."

"And the second thing?" asked William.

"You will be presented with a choice."

"What choice?" William was surprised. He had been given none all this time.

"You'll know when the time comes. For now, focus on the principles of your downfall," Milena replied, "The idealism Ahmed's father and your own grandfather has passed onto you is a noble one; there's no denying it. But it lacked a crucial and substantial understanding; that this current world does not care about noble intentions or principles. *They* don't give a shit. You die, you live; it only matters to *them* when it suits *their* design. *Their* main goal is always to enrich themselves more and more, always to win, no matter what the cost. Their domination machinery and its parts are the ultimate monster, evolved over time to force its way through fear, manipulation and greed, using religion, media and money. Who do you think is behind all this fighting among nations for hundreds of years? Who benefits from your misery and your continuous hate for one another? They've been doing it so effectively and for so long that you accept it as the norm, with no possible alternative. They destroyed those who value honor or pride. They laugh at your so-called dignified struggle. You must leave that misguided pride behind and see things in all their clarity. That what you call 'the way of the world' is one big, long con. The most sophisticated con in the entire history of your kind," said Milena and continued, "Your fight shouldn't be beating them at their own game but to change the game. Destroy it until its foundations will lie in a pool of rubble. That is the only way."

Ahmed's face grew inexplicably darker as William continued to listen. Unable to make sense of it, William decided to ignore it. "I think I understand. But I don't know how to do it or even if it's doable," he said.

"You have what it takes to figure out the *how* part; it's already in you, William. You had it all along. Buried deep beneath your mind, clouded by your depression and self-pity. All you need is a push. And I am that push which will make you move. You'll see in the end," said Milena.

"But how can all this be my fault? Why am I paying the price here?"

"It's not just your fault, it's everyone's fault. Everyone who blindly accepts this design is guilty of ignorance. You, my dear William, are paying for the sins of all."

"Oh, now I'm Jesus Christ, am I?"

"No. You're not. I never met Jesus or heard of him except from your kind. I have been around for thousands of years; believe me, I would have done. But I know a Paul. Very clever guy," she said with a strange smile and a wink, "Also, dying for the sins of mankind without any visible outcome is pointless. You, my friend, just have to live the agony of the billions alive today to be one of them, so that your words can resonate through them. Experience always beats knowledge. What you knew or saw wouldn't be enough to vibrate at the same frequency as those fallen ones. This price you refer to is to serve a greater purpose. The greatest purpose of all."

"To save mankind…" said William with a hint of mockery.

"Yes, it is, even though you still don't believe in it."

"So what now? How does this nightmare end? Are we not done yet?"

"Not quite. Before we move on to our next destination, we need to complete this one. It's now time for you to choose."

"Tell me, Milena, I'm ready. Let's finish this already," said William confidently, hoping to end it with whatever needed to be done.

Ahmed gave him a sinister smile like he'd been waiting for this moment from the beginning. His lips were cracked and bleeding, his teeth were now crooked and dirty yellow, drooling repulsively.

"I hope you are. This is going to be a hard one," Milena said, "Check in your other pocket."

William reached in his left pocket. His fingers touched a piece of cold metal and the box of mints. He knew straightaway what the metal was. He pulled it out and gently held it.

"A gun? What for?" he asked. He no longer sounded as confident.

"This is the instrument of your choice, William. You'll all die here; that's certain. How painful it will be lies in your hands," Milena answered coldly, "There are only three bullets in that gun. Not enough for all of you. If you choose to kill yourself, you will simply pass on to our next destination. But your wife and children will drown here in the next tide. If you kill them, they won't have to suffer that long and painful death, only you will. Now choose."

"No, no, no, you cannot ask this of me! It's not fair. What's the point of it? What possible lesson will I learn from this choice?" asked William, taking a step back. Even his body was protesting.

"It's a test of character. Not a test to satisfy me but a test to see who you are. Can you do the unthinkable if it's going to spare your family or will you simply cut and run?"

"What if I did? They're not even my real family. What if I just shot myself and save myself the suffering?" asked William, "And why doesn't this asshole do it?"

"Because I'm already dead, you stupid fuck. I'm at the bottom of this dark sea, feeding the sharks," Ahmed said. Now his face looked more decomposed, "Let me refresh your memory."

William may have sensed what was about to happen again, but he still couldn't duck fast enough to escape Ahmed's swipe at his forehead.

He was now Ahmed, in the darkness of the night, under torrential rain, trying with all his strength to row over the swells toward a single point of light on the horizon. He didn't even know if it was another boat or a lighthouse; all he knew was he had to reach that light. The lives of his family depended on it.

Suddenly Malika screamed; her mother was about to tip over the gunwales.

"Baba, Baba, come quick, she's falling!"

In a panic, Ahmed rushed over and pulled his wife back up. She had slipped and nearly fallen overboard while trying to catch the cover as it was blown to the other side. If Ahmed had been a tad too late, Malika's weak arms would have let go. Yousef, in the meantime, was trying to tie the cloth to secure it.

But this heroic rescue caused an unfortunate result. As Ahmed was trying to rescue his wife, the oars had slid into the sea. They were still quite close, but as Ahmed reached out to grab them, before they were lost for ever, a high wave slammed into the boat and flung him overboard.

"Baba, baba!"

"Ahmed!" his panicking family yelled.

William felt Ahmed's terror. Choking in the salt water. He drowned in that raging sea along with Ahmed.

"Enough, enough, please," William begged on his knees, coughing and terrified, "I can't take it anymore, I want it to end, now!"

"That is entirely up to you my dear William. Know that I will not judge you; only you can judge yourself," Milena replied. She sounded sincere, "The question is, are you willing to live your life knowing that in an alternate reality, your wife and children died slowly, terrified, watching one another as the light in their eyes faded, lungs filling with salt water, screaming, and you nowhere to be found…"

William felt his blood curdle. His body was racked with involuntary tremors. This was his biggest fear. Witnessing the death of his children. He recalled that first time he had looked at Charlie's face. His firstborn. At that moment, a horrific thought had ruined that peaceful ecstasy right when he was lost in his son's innocent eyes.

What if he died? Oh, God, I beg of you, I pray to you, with all my heart and being. Please never let me see his blood drained from his body, never let me caress his cold and white skin… Take my life and spare me this, O mighty God… Never test me with my baby's loss… he remembered thinking.

And now, he was confronted with his biggest fear, and asked to do the deed himself…

"How long do I have?" asked William, his eyes filling. The gun trembled in his hand.

"You have to decide now, William," Milena answered in a calm, yet firm tone.

"Will they see me? Will they feel anything?"

"No, that would be the opposite of what we're talking about here."

"And what exactly are we talking about, Milena?"

"A kindness, William; we are talking about a kindness."

"Oh, God, help me…" sighed William, looking up to the heavens.

"He won't answer you, William; he never did. You were, and are, on your own. Besides, you don't need him or anyone else; you have everything it takes to decide to do anything you have to do. You have your mind, your morals, your soul, and your own strength. Stop relying on unseen deities and take the reins of your choices. Whatever you choose, you are the one who will have to live with the consequences, not God, not anybody else; you and you alone," Milena interrupted his prayers, "It's time, William, another wave is coming."

William looked at the frozen woman and children. He saw his own family. He began to tremble violently. Closing his eyes, he raised his head. He imagined them screaming in fear in an unknown language. Hugging one another, the mother trying to protect her children, the choking, the terrified breaths, the gurgle of water flooding their mouths. He remembered the children who died in that mud hut in Afghanistan. He felt sick.

Where is God when you need him? he wondered, *Maybe he really had nothing to do with it; maybe it's simply our own doing, after all… They're not even my real family, this is too much for one man, what have I ever done to deserve this torture… Just a bullet between the eyes or under the jaw and I'm home free, that's all… You're not responsible for this, this is not your burden to carry…*

"No! I can't!" he shouted.

"Can't what?" Milena asked.

William sat up straight, his face stone cold. Clenched his teeth and held the gun to his head. Then he put it in his mouth.

"Go ahead; you deserve it. You don't owe anything to these people. They're not even your real family," Ahmed said to William.

William only replied in vowels.

"This is not your fault; none of this is your fault. You had to see for yourself and now you have. It's time to move on. Why should you suffer? These people are strangers," Ahmed whispered in his ear, "You've paid your dues, William. Go ahead, spare yourself."

For a second, his finger started to press the cold trigger.

"Get on with it! You know the alternative. Do you really think you can bear that? Do it, spare yourself!" William's eardrums hurt; the shout was so loud.

He stopped, pulled the saliva-coated gun out of his mouth and whacked his own head three times. The blows broke the skin and turned his white hair red. He grunted as though possessed by the Devil himself. Then he broke into a wail.

"Take it all in, William," Milena said, "Take it all in so you never forget. This happens. This is real for millions of people. Take it all in… The misery, the utter hopelessness, the darkness within… "

He placed the gun on the deck and pressed his hand firmly on it. He winced where he stood for a while; next, with a sniffle, he shook his head several times like a wet dog. He stood up, holding the gun loosely. His trembling ceased at once. Gripping the gun, he took resolute steps toward the frozen people. He was clenching his teeth so hard that he could have shattered them. He was hyperventilating, which made him dizzy.

First, he aimed at Fairuz's forehead. An inexpert – yet point-blank – shot that caught the top of the skull instead. It shattered her skull, swallowing her left eye and part of her nose. He didn't stop to inspect the gory wound, terrified of being unable to recognize his wife.

Without a pause, he pointed the gun at Yousef.

"You still have two bullets left, William. You can still get out of this. One is more than enough. Besides, isn't this what you dreamt of doing every morning? This one won't even be the ultimate end. You will only pass on to your next destination, alive and well," said a calm Ahmed, now undistinguishable from a zombie, decomposed flesh dangling in tatters and everything.

"Baba, where are we going?" William remembered – as Ahmed once again – Yousef's voice as they were leaving their home.

"We're going to Europe, son. It's not safe here anymore. We'll make a new life there."

"What about my toys, my stuff?"

"We have to leave them here, son. We'll get new ones later," he had said, his eyes filling up, knowing it would take a miracle to get the same things again.

"And Malika? Is she leaving her dolls here too?"

"Yes, son, she's leaving them too. We'll get her better ones," Ahmed was trying to keep the trembling out of his voice, trying to avoid bursting into tears in front of his son.

"Can we go to Italy, Baba? I want to see the cathedrals," Yousef had asked innocently.

"Yes, Yousef, of course, son. In fact, Italy's really close to where we will land. We'll go there after Greece and I'll take you to see all the cathedrals there."

"And Rome, Baba, I want to see Rome too. I want to see where the gladiators fought."

"And Rome… Of course."

"Promise, Baba?"

"I promise Yousef; I promise a Baba promise."

"I'm sorry, I'm so sorry, son," said William said to the frozen boy, "I couldn't keep it, I just couldn't, forgive me, forgive me…" and fired the gun straightaway, from a distance this time. He didn't want to shatter his son's lovely face too.

He had missed the forehead; the shot went into the neck. Thick, sticky blood splashed his face. His tongue felt for the warm blood trickling down his upper lip and licked. He wanted to keep a part of his alternate son with him for ever, like a memento.

Then a terrible uncertainty fell upon him. *What if he won't die?* he thought for a second. *What if the shot to the neck won't be enough and he'll suffer a slow death?*

His every muscle, even the ones he didn't know existed were shaking as if he were being electrocuted.

"Don't worry, William, he's gone…" Milena comforted him in a calm, sweet voice.

Turning to Malika, William placed the muzzle on her forehead; he couldn't take any chances now. Under the pressure, the skin around that point paled.

"Only one bullet left. Are you sure you can go through with it? How can you do this to our little girl, you monster! How can you do this to our little baby after we just saved her?" a disgusted Ahmed asked before those rotting hands grabbed William's forehead once again.

William found himself in a refugee camp behind the Turkish border. Fairuz was screaming:

"Ahmed, Ahmed, run, run, Malika's gone, they got her, they got her! Go, run, save her!"

Watching Ahmed run like hell towards the exit, William followed. Ahmed reached the exit and was yelling at a group of people – two customs officers and three civilians dressed in baggy trousers. Grabbing Malika, who'd been standing in the middle, looking distraught, he ran away, carrying her. William was able to hear what they were saying as they approached him.

"Baba, they said they were taking me to the children's playground, I wanted to tell you, but they said I had to come quickly or other children would take my place; I'm sorry, Baba," she wept.

"Never, ever leave my side again, Malika, do you understand me, never again!" Ahmed yelled, making her cry harder. William felt Ahmed's terrified guilt.

"Malika, I'm sorry for shouting, I was scared, there are bad people here, I thought I lost you, my little girl, I was scared, I'm sorry. I mean it, though: never ever leave my side again!"

"I won't, Baba; I promise," she said sniffling and wiping her tears.

"And now, after we rescued her from those pimps, you have the nerve to kill her with your own hands, huh? I don't know which is worse: her being sold to fat hairy pedophiles and penetrated over and over again or her own father shooting her without remorse," Ahmed said to William, now back on the boat with his gun placed on frozen Malika's forehead.

William was on the verge of mental collapse, he could barely stand up, now covered in a cold sweat all over.

"Shut up, just shut the fuck up!" William exploded.

"Might as well sold her with your own hands, you disgrace of a father!" Ahmed shouted back, "You still have a way out, William. It'll only take a second; just put the gun in your mouth again, pull the trigger and you'll be free. It's that easy," he whispered in his ear again.

William flashed him a revolted look. Ahmed looked more like a corpse than a man now.

With a noise between a laugh and a cry like a zebra felled by a lion, eyes averted, William cocked the gun again. Just when he was about to shoot, he turned his head for a look and saw the dimple on Malika's chin. It was in the same place as Candice's. The cute little dimple they used to pretend was a deep valley as his fingers walked on it like a headless puppet when she was little.

"And now, famous alpinist Dr. Climbhobble meets his greatest challenge yet, the absolutely magnificent Candice Valley. Great glory awaits if he can reach the other side!"

William's mind resounded with Candice's giggles at that announcement and the fingers struggling with that tough climb. He thought he could hear her sweet three-year-old voice.

"Last chance…" said corpse Ahmed.

One of the fat tears falling down William's chin hit a spark that came out of the gun in mid-air; they fused, canceling each other.

There was no one to witness the spine-chilling scream filling the frozen sky. The demented wailing of a man bearing the combined laments of four fathers.

"You're very brave, William," Milena said, "Now it's time to end this."

William didn't notice the wind rising and the waves pounding the boat again.

The world resumed spinning, but he remained frozen in time. Still trapped in those memories with Candice's giggles mixed with Yousef's innocent dreams of gladiators.

William turned to look at Ahmed, who had regained his former appearance and had a warm smile. Then he vanished.

A ten-feet-high wave overturned the boat, trapping William under it. He did not struggle, instead, he let go and embraced his coffin. He wished the water wouldn't wash Yousef's blood from his face in his last moments.

And then, that old bright blinding light came. He was non-existent again for a moment.

CHAPTER 4
PERSONAE
NON GRATAE

The devil hides in plain sight. He divides his body into many pieces, each with its own unique task to serve the master. Every piece embodies one of the attributes of evil. Like the seven deadly sins, each operates in its own filth, promising everything we wish for, flattering our flesh, yet always aiming to feed one another's insidious and unholy agenda, only to reach and regroup at the top, where they merge into the perfect beast. The beast that feeds on our hate, our fear, our despair, and our alienation. It divides and conquers.

The devil hides in plain sight, among us, inside us, for it is legion…

I don't want to go on; I just want to die… I have no more hope or will to live… Nothing means anything anymore… It's all a lie. There's no purpose behind it all. We're merely breathing to die and breathing for the sake of living is not worth it…

I hate living… I want to die now…

Such were the first thoughts on William's mind as he opened his eyes. He had no need to look around to see that he was once again in that dark emptiness at the start of his journey with Milena. He was looking at his reflection on the shallow layer of water on the ground, lying down prone. He wouldn't want to look at himself either if he had only kept his eyes shut. This time, however, the face in that reflection looked alien. The man he was staring at was not even staring back. It was just the face of some stranger left without a shred of sanity. And the eyes: there was madness in those eyes. Albeit a peaceful one. A madness devoid of flame, a madness fully accepting its fate... Looking into them, he realized they belonged to someone not only lacking fear but also hope...

"It will pass, I promise. The hard part is over. You have suffered what you were meant to. It is over now," Milena said.

William didn't see her; he was still looking into those two crazy eyeballs, trying to understand what they displayed. Only darkness as far as he could see.

It was like looking into the abyss and waiting for the abyss to look back. A game of wills between two rivals.

"The things you experienced were not visions. They have all happened to you in other realities, as they did to countless people in this one. You're lucky to have them," Milena said.

William didn't lift his head to look at her, neither did he say anything back. He was entranced in his own distorted image.

The abyss, he thought, *it can't be all that's left. There must be something deep down there. A clue, a hybrid remnant of who I was and who I became.*

"It's there, William, but staring at it blindly won't reveal it. You must first process what you have lived and seen. You must read between the lines, search and find the causes that set things in motion in the first place. You must solve the puzzle," Milena said.

"I forget you can read my mind..." William spoke at last, "It was a little invasive at first but I'm past caring now. I have lived with you the worst things I could ever imagine. It's like you are a part of me now."

"I'm flattered, William," Milena said tenderly.

"Don't be. I still hate you," he said. His deranged grin received a mischievous one in response.

"I'm sorry for everything you had to go through, William. But it was all necessary. The greatest metamorphoses in history rose from agony. You needed that for our next step."

"You mean saving the world again, I guess?" asked William, his now darker gaze still searching for the end of the pit.

"Yes. It's time to start to shape the message," Milena answered.

"The message. Hmm, all right. My first message would be that the world is a fucked-up place with fucked-up people and a fucked-up system. Don't even try to do it. Opt out as soon as you can. How is that for a message, huh?"

"Perfect! Because it is the truth. But it is also the statement of the obvious. The message we need to communicate would present a new way, a better way, not just for some but for all. That is what's valuable; that is what we must achieve," enthused Milena.

"I have no idea what your new way could be. Or even give a shit. I just killed my kids with my own hands. I'm not sure you understand my state of mind at the moment. I'm truly, utterly and terribly not here anymore. I'm gone and I don't even know where I am or why I'm there. I'm not present anymore. So don't expect me to be eager to save a world for people I hate. But for whatever it's worth, please, do tell; I do like hearing your voice," he said, sounding and looking more insane than ever since setting off on a journey with this beautiful creature. He recalled something she had said earlier: "You will dance on the edge of madness."

"Oh, no, Pups. It is not my place to tell you anything. I'm only here to guide you, not educate you. You'll find the answers by yourself. But don't worry, I will help you," she said calmly, "I told you when we first met, that we would debate; remember?"

"Yes, I do. You also said that I'd had only my pathetic self to debate with until then," he said with that wicked smile again.

"Yes, I did; but you are no longer pathetic. You have changed. That half-conscious, insecure and depressive guy has been forged in a fire blended by grievous pain and suffering, to rise as a man from blood-soaked lessons, a man of steel and clarity in purpose. Both in his mind and his soul. This conversation will be much more interactive than what you'd had with your choked, terrified mind, and much more fruitful, I guarantee you."

"Wow, what a pep talk!" he mocked, "Before I met you, I was depressed and joyless, but still had hope. Now I'm utterly wretched, in the dark."

"No, you are not. You're more awake than you have ever been. You'll see it once the effects pass," Milena replied, "Look, William. I know you think you've been tortured and hounded, but it was all for your own good. You had to know, not in a sense of mind but know it in your heart, that these things are happening. They are real. They are happening. Without really knowing, how can you find the answers to beat them? Everything our journey comprises is, and will be, for your benefit; this I promise you. Now get a hold of yourself and clear your head. We still have a long way to go. Time is of the essence."

"What more do you want from me?" asked William plaintively.

"I want you to become who you were meant to be. I want you to crash so that your outer shell fractures and your inner light can shine from the cracks and eventually, shatter that shell into pieces to free the rays of wisdom in order to illuminate this darkened world."

"Boy, you really know how to talk to a guy! Are you going to blow me up once more or shall we start? Before I decide to kill myself…"

"Ha-ha, as you wish, my liege," she chuckled sweetly, "Perfect; let's get down to it then."

Those Insidious Bastards

"All right, let the games begin. So let's commence with the most obvious but the broadest question. Let's brainstorm and see where the chips fall. What is wrong in the world that led you and your loved ones to go through those terrible things?" Milena asked.

"Everything's still fuzzy in my mind. All floating around in random. I need time to process… "

"Which we don't have, William. Try to gather your thoughts and memories of your experiences while they are still fresh. Let me help you find a starting point. What was the main theme in them all?"

"I'll try my best but I'm so confused right now," William said and continued, "Let's see… I think there was no common theme in all of them but a mixture. A mixture of blind belief, immoral and dishonest people, people full of hate, full of desire, people lacking empathy."

"Go on, what else?"

"If I were to say one thing, it would be that people are being led to hate, despise and mistreat one another when someone stands in their way or if they seek power. But why? Is it solely ego? Where does this hate come from? How can a wolf dress in sheep's clothing without anyone twigging? Why does nobody empathize with anyone else?" he asked himself. Memories were now floating rapidly towards his mouth.

"Can it have been by design?" Milena asked, "And do you think this wickedness applies to all of humankind?"

"I'm not sure yet; it may have been designed all right but how? And no, it doesn't apply to us all. There are good and honest people out there too. A lot actually. But they are afraid. Afraid of being hurt by the wicked ones. So they stay quiet, they keep their heads down and don't interfere with what's happening all around." He then added, "The only thing necessary for the triumph of evil is for good men to do nothing…"

"Well said. You know that I'm aware this quote doesn't belong to you, right?"

"Of course; I would never presume to trick a demon," William gave a slick smile.

"Very funny! It was just an expression, stop it already," she smiled back with a slow, teasing swipe at his arm like a girl hell-bent on seducing him.

"Yeah, yeah, right. OK, back to business. So the good guys are afraid of the terrible things the bad guys are willing to do. That is why they stand down, keep themselves to themselves and avoid any conflict whatsoever most of the time. Until…" said William. His desperation was slowly giving way to another familiar emotion: Anger.

"Until?" Milena asked.

"Until trouble finds its way to them…" William replied, "But then it's too late to stand their ground. Evil is turned on and united. Organized. But these are mindless cogs in a much greater design. These minions only collect the scraps. They are the street thugs, the mafiosi, the money-crazed brokers, and titans of industry. They are small potatoes to be sacrificed and replaced at a moment's notice. They're not aware of who or what they truly are serving." The things his mind spewed were surprising. "They're just pawns in a global chess game that's been fixed for centuries. Their masters are hiding behind the curtain of modern life and dogma."

"Very good. And who do you think these puppeteers might be?" Milena asked.

"The privileged one-percenters. The ultra-rich and powerful of the world." *Except, something was missing,* he thought.

"Dive deeper, William."

"No, not those, they too are the instruments of the real villains," he hastened, realizing he was onto something now. "The real evil poses as gentlemen, noble chosen, saviors and liberators. They are the kings and queens of this world, the world shapers, the war bringers, the money creators. They are the real dominators over us."

"Name them, William, name them!" she challenged him once again.

"The queens and kings, sheiks, patriarchs, religious leaders, media moguls, oil barons, big pharma, high-tech tycoons, patrons of finance, banks of the world..." William's words were sprouting like machine gun bullets. Fast, straight, powerful – and deadly.

"And how do they shape it all? What are their methods?"

"They use religion to numb the masses, they use media to manipulate them, they use money to enslave them, social media to blind them and with the coming result of it all, with people's ignorance, they dominate them. Without them even knowing it. They target our flesh to consume our spirits."

"How? Be more specific; pour out the skeletons in the closet."

"It's all a scheme. A scheme with the motivation of power at its core. Money is created to divide us, mass media to pump hate in our hearts against one another and divide us. They work in sync. They turn us into depraved consumers by marketing us things we don't need, so we stay in constant need of money. They shroud our minds with irrelevant religious rules, put fear in our hearts disguised as divinity. They divert our attention from social injustice and their crimes with celebrities, high life and psychical demonstrations of the flesh," William said and continued, "How did we fall so far from the Newtons and the Platos, who searched the secrets of the universe and existence, to be these dancing, ass-displaying, duck-lipped monkeys, who surf on top of moving cars and eat detergent pods as social media challenges. Humans used to challenge nature, the gods, the unknown. Now we challenge one another to see who can be the biggest imbecile. Knowledge used to be power. Now it's the biggest ass and boobs."

"Very good, William. We are on the right track," Milena said.

"Nobody feels valuable any longer. They don't create anything, not anything of real value at least. They work in cubicles all day just to buy a shirt with a bird or a horse on it. Work in the modern world has become rowing in a slave galley; no one knows where they're headed or why, they just pull and push to get their reward: money. Money, which, in fact, has no value in itself. If more slaves are needed, the more money they create and more pointless goods to spend it on. With every buy, limited-time satisfaction is guaranteed. And indeed, limited it is. Once it wears off, it turns into despair and you need more money to regain that rapture. It's the biggest addiction pandemic that has ever been in history and we don't even recognize it. Consumer goods have become the greatest and most variable drugs in the world and everyone needs a regular fix. A vicious cycle. It's ingenious. Who needs insidious self-aware robots to imprison us in a Matrix-like dream world, when we enslave ourselves voluntarily. And the system is basically a global Ponzi scheme. They just create money out of thin air and with it, interest rates. This way, they can always increase the amount of money to finance their slave galley. And it's all going to crash and burn soon," said William. He was like someone under the influence of an unknown power. All that had been on the tip of his tongue for years, but which he couldn't find the right words for until now, fell from his mouth in a powerful cascade. "But money is not their end goal. Their main goal is to dominate and oppress. That's why they need distractions and other kinds of sedatives to keep us occupied and numb. That's where media and religion come into the picture. Religion to divide us and fear one another, media to manipulate us into hating one another."

"They're so afraid of you uniting under a banner of just humanity that they keep racism alive, invent holy crusades, create false monsters, and crown mediocrity. They ignite senseless wars, foment chauvinism, do everything in their power to divide you. They don't want you to reach your supreme selves… Enlightened and conscious. Anyone who thinks they are free harbors the biggest delusion in the history of the world. You have never been more chained." She could have been echoing what was on his mind.

"Exactly… And it's only going to get worse. Soon, most jobs in the world will be done by machines, like you said before. What's going to happen to all those unemployed people? How will they live?" asked William as if talking to himself. She had mentioned the same thing a while back. It still made little sense.

"Think, William, think. You have the answer. What is about to change the world very soon? What fundamental social change is being vetted for you right this moment? Think, you have it!"

He pondered for a moment. The answer was at the tip of his tongue. He could almost hear it. Then it struck him like a bolt of lightning.

"Artificial reality! Yes, that's it. It's their next phase in our slavery design. They will transfer us to fake worlds, so we won't be a hindrance to their new order. They will put us into a coma. What sleeps doesn't rebel... But wait!" said a panicked William, "That's not all. It is only one of the countless benefits. They won't leave us alone in our dream world. No, sir. We'd be costing them; they'd be expecting payment. They got us by the balls, why release us now? They'll no longer have to hook us on material goods, because it's all going to be on codes. With one click, they'll be able to produce anything we want to consume, much cheaper than it is now. Of course, as long as we keep paying. And as payment, they will use us as their servants both in real life and in that fake world. They'll keep us on hold as their flesh–and–bones army, ready to be deployed at a moment's notice. We will be so addicted to that artificial world that we'll work in real life as they please so we can get back to that world. The so-called Metaverse will be the new heroin. But this time, every one of us will be hooked on it and not just some of the unfortunate. Why use machines that would cost when they have free slaves a-plenty? We'll do everything they ask, our only reward a fake world they control the access to. Food and a stacked shelter will be enough to sustain us, enough to keep us alive and breathing. They could feed us insects in real life if they wanted to and no one would protest. We'll all do everything that a drug addict does to get their fix today, all the inhuman and disgraceful things they are willing to do. And we cheer them for it."

"Bravo, William, you're on the verge of erupting like a volcano and immolating everything around just so you can create something new on the ashes. You understand the problem. You see the wickedness and insidious intentions that are designed for your fellow humans. But do you have the solution? How will you be able to wake up? What will replace this order that would really work?"

"We need to get rid of this cabal and its minions," declared William confidently, "Exposing them is not enough. They have been exposed many times before, only to come out the other side as victims of a conspiracy theory. What we need to do is to present a new way. A way in which every life matters, a way in which justice, honesty and decency reign supreme. A way people are ruled by conscious and enlightened leaders. A way everyone can live in prosperity and add value to their environment."

"What would be the first step to create such an order? What would be the preliminary condition?"

William reflected on all that he had seen and experienced, rapidly put it all in order and looked for the answer, murmuring like a schoolboy who had just learned finger counting. It popped out of nowhere like a penny dropped on the sidewalk.

"The right education!" he yelled, utterly certain, "An education based on morals, ethics and virtues."

"At long last! Come along, then. I want to show you something. You're ready," she said with a pleased grin.

A Precarious Dream

No flashes came this time. Nor any sensation of non-existence. The darkness surrounding them lifted gradually. Faint images started to emerge: of people walking, sitting on benches, children laughing. He saw a wondrous city glowing under a glorious sunshine. A city of symmetry and picturesque beauty formed around them. A city of divine proportions, full of serene people, far from the harsh, sullen faces William left behind. This city reminded him of *The Jetsons* he loved to watch as a kid.

"Where are we?" asked William, astonished.

"We, Pups, are in your hometown, in the year 2122. This, William, is what can be."

William wondered at his surroundings. There were people all around, talking, writing, painting, and reading. The buildings all seemed to be similar in height, shape and architectural design. There were roads but they were not busy. All the cars were the same. They had no drivers. Elevated trains whizzed overhead. There was movement everywhere, but no chaos or noise pollution. Everyone could hear everyone, no one was trying to outpace anyone, no one was in a rush. It was, all in all, peaceful.

"This, William, is all because of you," Milena said.

"Me? How?" asked William.

"This is the result of your actions, if you choose to spread your message born out of this journey."

"I don't know what message I can relay. Or how to do it, even if I knew. I'm not a leader, Milena; I'm not one of those revolutionary guys in history, whose bloods burn with incinerating fire," William said shyly.

"You don't have to be. You just need to pave the way, William. Do you think everything you see here happened in your lifetime? It took many people to figure out how to achieve it. But it was only possible with your words. You, William, are not the executive of this new world but you are its unofficial messiah. Not appointed by God or ordained as a holy man but as a human, who showed the courage to resist and expose the system that oppressed your fellow men, refused the dogmas that were imposed on you, defied the fear they chained you by, and only delivered your words to eager ears. Your task is not to solve the mechanics of this new order. Your task is to ignite and guide those who will. You're here to set this new world thesis in motion. But I will give you some pointers to work with; don't worry." A big yellow eye winked as one corner of her lip lifted. William realized he still couldn't get over her indescribable beauty. His eyes shone every time he looked at her. "But first, tell me: what do you see here? Ask, if you have any questions."

He looked around for any resemblance to his own world. It all looked standardized in a totally alien manner.

"I always thought we'd have flying cars in the future…"

"No need. These people are not as mobile as you. Terrestrial vehicles are more than enough for their daily needs. They have the tech to do it, they just prefer not to. They love to watch the sky in all its beauty and serenity."

"Why is everyone dressed pretty much the same, except for colors? And what about the cars: they are all the same! And buildings! How can they all be the same design and construction?" asked William.

"Good observation. Well, this world's mantra is harmony, William. Harmony in everyday life, harmony in possessions, harmony among people, harmony of all life. No one has a more luxurious lifestyle than anyone else. Everyone lives more or less in similar spaces. Of course, there are some differences; not enough to cause envy, though. That's why the buildings look the same. It's the same principle in the countryside. Houses there are very similar too," she explained, "As for cars: they belong to everyone. They belong to people, each and every one of them. They're all autonomous. Whoever needs one for transport just grabs one. There's enough for everyone. If a bottleneck occurs or if someone has farther to go, they hop on the train. The same applies to clothes. No one dresses to show off here; they simply dress to cover the body. People in this world are too busy to waste time in front of mirrors to decide what to wear in order to impress. Besides, impressing someone here takes talent far beyond mere ostentation."

"Interesting. I wonder how they overcame their narcissistic impulses, though. It's against our nature…"

149

"What is your nature, William?"

"We talked about this before, remember? Humans are greedy and envious… We have an insatiable need to surpass and gain superiority over one another. We are infamous for it. It's called ambition," said William.

"There is no envy here, only introjection. No greed, only longing for success. People here also endeavor to surpass one another. Not in possessions or physical beauty, though; in talent, achievements and creations."

"But how can they restrain impulses carved into their DNA for millions of years? Humans had to kill or be killed in their primitive state. That urge stayed with us in modern times too, with stepping on others for money and title!"

"What money?" Milena asked with another cute grin.

"What money? Money! What makes the world go round. What people kill one another for. What successful people earn to make others their servants. What do you mean what money?!" asked an incredulous William.

"There is no money here, William. They don't need it. There are no banks or bankers, no financial system of any kind."

"Wait a minute! You want me to understand – or better yet – believe that people here live in prosperity without money? What about the economy, production, taxes, government budget… I mean, who pays for all this?" He seemed too confused to manage anything other than mumbling, which made Milena chuckle.

"Look around you. Do you think this age needs people to produce or build anything? It's all done by machines here. Technology had advanced enough to supply clean energy for free, autonomous machines that work for people, incredible computing capabilities needing no human effort to sustain life. Well, except for the creation of it, of course. Technology and energy belong to the people, to them all. These people are both creators and consumers. They build machines to produce what they need and consume. What they truly value is creativity, though. Not to create money, wealth or things to feed their material needs, but to feed their souls and minds, and the pursuit of science to solve the mysteries of the universe. Everyone here is either an artist, a scientist or a philosopher," she said.

"But who governs it all? I mean, who decides how to distribute the resources?"

"People are still governed as the same way they were in your time. By elected people. The difference here is that the elected officials are virtuous. They have received further education, well above minimum standard – which already is quite high, by the way – in order to govern well. That is a *sine qua non*. And when I say educated, I don't mean only in sciences or social disciplines. The education system here is quite different from yours. It is what you proposed, in fact. It's founded on virtues. Honesty, ethics, honor, diligence, kindness, love, gratitude, patience, compassion, and above all, respect. Respect for one another. Respect for every living being. Every citizen of this world spends their first years assimilating these virtues, these principles. Only after this foundation is solidified come the sciences, arts and every other discipline," Milena replied, "In order to stand for election, a higher level of spiritual cultivation is essential. A higher level of wisdom and consciousness. The governors of this world do not see themselves as privileged individuals. They consider themselves responsible for their fellow humans. It is an obligation, a burden, which they take very seriously."

"Unbelievable! It's like utopia."

"Not like, it is utopia in action. This is no dream, William. This is a possible reality," Milena said, "And there are more than enough resources for everyone. Everyone gets enough for a comfortable life. Resources in your world were also more than enough. The problem was, some elite oppressors wanted to own most of them, while others worked endlessly in meaningless jobs for a fraction of the scraps. In here, no one is filthy rich, no one is poor. No one envies another's possessions. They know that everyone loses in a system where only some get the most of everything."

"But what if someone tries to get more than their fair share? What if someone wants to be privileged? To live in a bigger house? To have a boat? I can't simply believe that human nature has fundamentally changed in a hundred years!"

"It is a possibility, of course. Somewhere along the line, some pompous asshole with primitive coding may come and demand more, just because he contributed more, he is cleverer than most or worked harder. But the thing is, this system will reject him. He'll be cold shouldered. Because people here are generally raised to be far more noble-minded in matters of rights and material motivation than in your world. It all depends on who holds power, you see. Remember me saying there's no right, there's no wrong, there's only power? Let me elaborate: it's not just a cliché, it has a much deeper meaning than it sounds. Power doesn't necessarily mean domination over people. That was your interpretation. Power is just power. It can be righteous, it can be oppressive and selfish. A hundred years ago, in your time, the majority of people were only aware of advantage, material gain, possession, and domination. Because your misguided democracy and money-based system crowned these values as merits. Here, on the other hand, people crown knowledge; they value spiritual development and respect for everyone and everything."

"You mention respect more than any other. What about love? Shouldn't love be above respect?"

"Not here, William. Love is good; it's divine and powerful. But respect is transcendent. It's the glue that holds everything together. There can be no love without respect; that would only be obsession. But respect can exist without love. Respect for yourself, your fellow humans, everything there is and will be. Respect is harmony, William," said she calmly.

"I remember you saying 'fuck love' before. Now you call it divine?" asked William.

"That was a different argument altogether. Love is divine, yes but it won't solve your problems. That's what I meant before."

"OK, OK, don't get mad!"

"How can I get mad at you, my silly monkey?" she said with a smile.

"I never thought I'd find being called monkey cute," he replied with a smile of his own, "As for respect, I think I understand what you are saying. It makes sense. What about God? Does he exist in this world?" He wasn't sure which answer he wished to hear.

"Yes, God is present here too. But not in form the way you imagined it back then. God here is not vengeful or angry. He does not punish. He creates the cosmos and sets you free. Free to find the holiness in yourself, not in their *Holinesses* of flesh and bone. Here, people search for God everywhere: in nature, in the cosmos, in themselves, not in churches or mosques. There are no middlemen or human-shaped constructs between God and them, therefore, no organized religion. For them, God is the ultimate secret of it all, the last frontier of men's pursuit for intellectual superiority and spiritual enlightenment," she explained. William was pleased.

"So religion is forbidden then?"

"No, it's not. There are still some people who practice the old religions. No one judges them; no one holds their belief over another's. It is, all the same, practically gone. Something that happened naturally. As humans progressed, they tended less and less to follow dogmatic words blindly. Logic and reason reign supreme here, not superstition," Milena replied, "Hardly anything is forbidden in this new world. People are free to find their own way. But if someone is lost entirely, society may exclude them. Not in a harsh way of course. They still get respect and compassion, although they do struggle to fit in the harmony of the collective. Respect comes with tolerance, you see."

"And who replaced the saints of old? Revolutionaries?"

"No one is canonized here. No human idols or saints; just past revolutionaries who loved others and worked for the good of the collective. They are commemorated, but not worshipped like demigods. No one sits on a throne here; no one's image is printed to be hung on walls. People know their ancestors and their saviors, the visionaries who made this world a reality. They appreciate, and are grateful for, the sacrifices made. But they don't worship those visionaries. You are remembered and respected above all," replied Milena.

A blushing William asked, curious, "What about crime? Laws, for that matter? You said nothing is forbidden here? How does that work?"

"I said hardly anything is forbidden, not nothing. Of course, there are laws and police forces to enforce them. But laws here are much simpler. Anyone who commits a crime against a fellow citizen is duly tried, judged and incarcerated if necessary. The main difference is crimes are not what they used to be. Murder, manslaughter, theft, arson, breaking and entering, rape, and hard drug use are still crimes. But let me assure you, with the right education and creature comforts available to all, they're very rare. Even a fistfight here is huge news, and is usually caused by people with mental issues. They're only punished if they cannot be treated. In any case, a criminal mind could never find a place among these people."

"What about naysayers? Can people freely criticize their governors, the system?"

"Freedom of speech and exchange of ideas are respected as fundamental rights. There is no censorship here, quite the opposite: sharing ideas is actively encouraged. People here love to debate and find common ground. Philosophy is embedded in primary education," explained Milena.

"What about alcohol?" asked William shyly, hoping there was still some around.

"A-ha, you mean partying, I guess. Boys will be boys, right?" she laughed. "Well, alcohol is still free. But people here are much more responsible. They know their limitations and when to stop. They also have instant sober-me-up pills. No more drunk and disorderly, no more hangovers. Wouldn't that have been a treat in your time?"

"And how! Those pills would've spared my blushes many a time," he laughed back, "You said hard drugs are forbidden. Does that mean some drugs are legal here?"

She knew what he meant.

"You hope cannabis is free here, right, you dog?" she smiled.

"Yep. I never thought of it as a drug, anyhow."

"Yes, William, it is totally free here. In fact, nobody smokes cigarettes any longer, only cannabis. Besides, the best debates take place when high," she giggled.

"Hallelujah!" came the mischievous yell, "What about marriage? Children?"

"Marriage is considered an outdated custom, although everyone is allowed to marry. But most people simply choose to commit to each other without any restraints, not that there is still a legal regulation for it. They just choose to. The majority of people believe in free love and freedom in life. If someone's love for you is conditioned on possession, then it's not you that they truly love but their own selves; a love bathed in egoism," replied Milena.

"Freedom is loneliness," echoed Daniel's voice in William's head.

"Maybe; but so be it. Who said loneliness was bad?"

"I thrive in isolation. I love it. No one ever got why I do. I was called anti-social, introverted or even worse for it. But I always did my best when I was on my own. Alone in my thoughts. In my opinion, anyone who craves company is weak and not self-reliant."

"Don't be so harsh, William. Everyone needs a kindred soul now and then. But I agree with you. Solitude is good for creativity and self-enlightenment. These people do not associate freedom with loneliness. Their understanding of loneliness is not as bitter as yours. For them, it means serenity," said Milena and continued, "As for children, they no longer belong to their parents. Every citizen here is responsible for raising the young and their well-being. Where there is collective righteousness, the more influence on the children, the better. Everyone is a parent to all; everyone is a child to all. You see, everyone here does everything for the betterment of the collective. This is the way they are coded. Nobody claims ownership of anyone else here."

"Huh, well, this is a surprise. I don't know how I could do that. I mean, my children are my most precious beings in the whole wide world. I can't imagine letting someone else teaching them values other than my wife and me," said William.

"That's because of your instinct of exclusivity over your offspring. It's how you were raised to think. Given how people live in your world, you're not wrong. Here, though, people share common and noble values, accepted by all with trust and respect for one another. They're more than happy to get help raising their most precious beings."

"Astonishing. And a little intimidating too, I must confess."

"Don't worry. You won't have to live through it in your life. Remember, you are already way in the past in this age," she gave a wry smile.

"I know…" sighed William. "What about romantic jealousy, though? What happens when someone doesn't love you back? So many terrible things were done on that account!"

"It's a probability, of course, but respect rules the heart. Unrequited love causes heartache but not violence," Milena replied.

"Let's get back to production, the economy, as I understand it. How does that work here? What about the media?"

"Well, think of it this way. As I said, production of goods no longer depends on human labor. And all the technology belongs to everyone. Once they attained the required level of technology, machines and robots did everything from production and agriculture, construction of infrastructure, factories, facilities, and property, and even everyday services. They're not owned by companies or an elite minority. So everyone can benefit fairly. Majority votes are used to decide on goods and services. Remember, people here are not entranced by material beauty or possessions. They do like to live well, of course, but they have a balanced concept of their needs. They need no fancy clothes or cars to show off; no desire for servants, ten thousand feet square homes to sleep in, gold-plated forks, or useless luxuries. What they crave instead is progress: knowledge, intellectual empowerment, arts, music, and talents. There's no money because everything they need is freely available. There is no shortage of goods. Energy here is not derived from fossil fuels; they use new types of clean and powerful energy sources, harnessing the energy of the sun, the wind, the oceans, even the hidden energies that surround the air they breathe. Health services are free for all, and most of it is also conducted by machines. Technological progress has cured most illnesses. No one dies due to lack of money any longer. As for the media, with virtuous people come unbiased and objective news. There no longer is propaganda or false news, only truth. Truth is not obfuscated from the masses as it was in your time."

"Unbelievable. This is everything I have ever dreamt of," said William.

"I know, that's why you are here."

"But, if no one works, what do they do all day?"

"What you call work doesn't exist here, that's true. But work doesn't mean chained to a computer in an office from nine to five, arguing in stressful meetings with no satisfactory goal or purpose or useful outcome. That was your slavery model. Here, everyone works to improve themselves in various disciplines. Sciences, social development, arts, music, philosophy, sports; everything that enhances life and enkindles greatness. From a very young age, they are guided towards disciplines they are capable of excelling in. But they are also free to choose what they want to focus on. That being said, discovering their strengths through scientific analyses and recommending appropriate areas has proved to be highly effective. Most of the time, they love what they do. If they don't, they may change direction. But they rarely reach their full potential if they don't follow the guidance they were given. This doesn't mean they fail; they just don't flourish. In any case, the norm is to do what you love. That way, what you call work is transformed into something they yearn to get up and continue in the morning. Work here is happiness, William."

"Do something you love and you won't have to work one day in your life," whispered William.

"Indeed. Another great quote from another wise man. You're a man after my own heart. Work should be for a noble cause. Not to crunch numbers to see how much something will cost and how much you can earn by selling it for a certain price, especially for trivialities. It makes people feel worthless: instant satisfaction for both parties that fades away the moment you reach your goal. This loop is a trap for your soul. An instantly numbing drug that keeps you needing more and more, until you realize on your deathbed that you spent your short time on this earth leaving nothing lasting or valuable to your name. The perfect recipe to destroy the spirit."

"I understand completely. It's made me wretched my whole life, took away all my motivation," said William, "This is the reason I have difficulty getting up from bed to start the vicious cycle all over again. This is the reason the dream of death gave me comfort all those nights before sleep. No one should have to feel like this. The loss of faith in a life worth living is a hell of our own making. It doesn't matter if it's imposed on us for centuries as the only way; we should know better. We are now conscious enough to perceive this fact."

"Oh, look at you... Are you the same man who questioned himself if he had what it takes to influence others? You look nothing like him," said Milena with a pleasant smile. He responded with a shy smile of his own, still not comfortable with such compliments. He was raised to believe he was never good enough. Never enough.

"Please don't flatter me; it's embarrassing," he said, blushing.

"I'm not. I told you, I have no reason nor any wish to lick your ass, I only speak the truth, whether it is harsh or pleasant. What is it with you and this misguided humility?

Humility is pride in disguise. If you have a good quality, you should be proud of it, embrace it, not vainly, but as justly deserved." Milena sounded as wise as a mentor.

"OK, OK, I get you, thanks. I'm just not used to praise, though," said William with a soft chuckle.

"You should be, and sooner than later, too. I did say time was of the essence," warned Milena. The speed of the change in her expression caused anxiety as well as arousal. *Weird*, he thought.

"I will do my best, I promise," he replied struggling to hide his blushes, "But let me first get back to something you'd mentioned before. That resources were enough for everyone. But what happens if advances in medicine lead to a massive drop in death rates and huge rise in overall quality of life with factors like stress, depression and poverty being things of the past. What if the population increases to much higher levels than it is now? How do they provide goods and services for massive numbers of people? What about living space?"

"William, there was never a shortage of resources and living space for much higher populations in your world either. The world is a very big cow with highly productive teats. It has always been. It was your greed and individual ambitions that prevented fair distribution. The day may come when there won't be enough to feed and provide for all, but that's not a problem now. You've already started to colonize other planets," she explained.

"But doesn't all this comfort make people lazy? Struggle and suffering are the pillars of greatness. You said it yourself: there is no path to greatness without great suffering. If everyone's born into comfort and has no need to work or strive like we used to, how do they improve themselves, how do they mature?"

"First of all, you are right. No man has become extraordinary without a defining milestone, be a failure or a great loss. Sorrow has been their fuel on their way to greatness. However, people here don't have to be as great as those men of your time. There were a handful of people who had the capacity to change the world back then. Even then, it was a never-ending battle to realize their goals. Here, everyone is given a chance to do extraordinary things. They don't need some awful setback to motivate them. They focus on greatness from the time they form their first words. Not with ambitions to get rich or rule a nation but to surpass themselves each day, unravel secrets and excel in every way. They don't need motivation; they have desire and discipline. Your mindset stuck in narrow views is no longer present. These people are self-reliant, self-disciplined and self-motivated, to expand their minds and enhance their reach in the universe."

"What if some are not? I mean, these people are still humans: we tend to stay in our comfort zones and be lazy. No education can suffice to change us all. And don't people get bored from all the peace and quiet?"

"There are some, of course. They still have the same rights as everyone. No one treats them harshly. But, in a society whose fundamental principles are righteousness and greatness, they can never find their rightful place. Sooner or later, they either fit in or just leave. It's like water and oil. They don't mix, ever. And no, they don't get bored at all. Contrary to popular belief, peace is not boring if you know how to party. And they do party, trust me," she said with a naughty smile.

"Milena, is the whole world like this now?"

"Unfortunately, not yet. You can't force change; you can only influence it. But most developed countries adapted this system, starting with educating a first generation and letting them pass it down to the next. But some so-called third world countries, especially those ruled by tyrants, resisted. Some of them had revolutions and succeeded in stepping into the new system but most failed to. The old system feeds the powerful, who held on to that power even if meant genocides at unprecedented levels of brutality. That being said, it is getting more and more unlikely for them carry on oppressing their people. Soon, they too will change their ways. It's just a matter of time," Milena answered.

"Why don't these people help them?"

"I told you, William, you cannot force change. Change has to follow its natural course. They must find their own way, make their own choices and fight for it, otherwise, they will always be subject to other people's mercy and rule. They need to free themselves, not be freed by others."

"What about the military? Do these people have one? Do they need one?"

"Of course they do. This new society is peaceful but not stupid. And they need the military. As I said, there are still primitive people – I mean, people stuck in your time – in the world, who want nothing more than to revert to the days of old, always looking for ways to get back to the old ways. They still need manpower for their military forces. Yes, there is technology to some extent, but nothing world threatening like before. Isolated from the majority of the world, and no match for the enlightened world (in scientific advances or access to resources) they don't keep people here awake at night. With very little natural resources left, those nations are swamped in poverty. The military here, moreover, benefits from the latest technology. They are so advanced that they can command and execute any battle plan from their living rooms, so to say. No one needs to die to defend their country. No more lost sons and brothers, no more anguish of war. By the way, there hasn't been a war for over fifty years now. All the developed countries that adapted the principles you gave birth to live in harmony and cooperation. This may sound strange to your understanding of your time, but believe me, once they found the way to harmony, once they understood that living for the betterment of the whole is the way to collective prosperity, every stone fell into place and everything changed."

"How can all this change happen in a mere hundred years? I still can't get my mind around it."

"Think back a hundred years, hell, just fifty years before your time. Think about the 1970s. Blacks and gays were still being persecuted. They were treated as thrash, sometimes killed for who they were. Women were not respected as intelligent individuals who had the brains for the workplace, except for typing. Any woman who chose to stand on her own two feet instead of cooking and raising children was considered marginal. Can these happen in your time now? Can these issues even be subject to debate in your world now? A lot can change in a hundred years, William, if people are willing."

"This is getting to be too much… Too much to take in. I have so many questions…"

"I know; but I think this is enough. As I said, the mechanics of this world is not your concern. I just wanted to show you how things can be. Believe me, it's possible. Anything is possible with enough people with a common purpose. You have the power to build your own heaven on earth. If you can create the hell you live in now, you can create this paradise too. It all depends on the courage and goodwill of the majority," Milena said, "We need to continue now."

"Wait, let me explore a little longer, please."

"All right, have a few moments to absorb it all."

"I still can't imagine how I can influence people to create this oasis. It sounds so inconceivable," said William hopelessly.

"All will be revealed soon enough, Pups..." she replied firmly.

"How about the nations that embraced the system? How did the powers that be react to this change? They must have done everything in their power to prevent it. Was there a hard revolution, was it bloody?" Hearing he was responsible for genocides in some hapless countries was upsetting; he had no wish to hear he had even more blood on his hands.

"You don't, William."

"I don't what?" Then it came to him. "You witch; I keep forgetting you can read my mind!" He smiled at her.

"I mean it. You're not responsible for any of the bloodshed. There is far less violence in the world now than there was before. All thanks to you," she consoled him.

"How about here, was it bad, the period of transition?"

"Let's just say that you can't make an omelette without breaking a few eggs," Milena replied, "Anyhow, this is not your concern now. No great change comes without sacrifice or pain either. But in the end, the outcome is worth all the upheaval and suffering. We must continue now, William."

"OK, just a few more minutes," he pleaded like a boy who was told they were leaving the playground.

"Fine, not too long, though," she replied like an affectionate mother.

William's inquisitive eyes examined the city, buildings and people, marveling at the harmonious scene.

I don't want to leave. I hate the idea of going back to that zoo after seeing this place. Why can't I be here in my lifetime? Why do I have to strive so others can live here? And do it for people I will never even meet? he thought.

But a moment later, it dawned on him: that was his ego talking. His individual, spoiled self.

I must be better than this. I must not give in to my selfish desires. This is the main cause of the hell world we live in. I must forsake myself, sacrifice for the betterment of my kin. This is the greatest cause a man can live for.

"I'm glad you think this way, William. Because you really will need the resolve."

He took this remark as a figure of speech.

Next, that potential paradise gradually faded away. William felt as wretched as he had on waking up that morning from that gratifying dream. Another world started to appear around him as paradise gave way to something far more ordinary.

CHAPTER 5
NOVO MODO

"Why couldn't we go through places such cushy before?" William complained.

"They had to be the way they were. It was part of the process," Milena teased.

"You and your processes!" He smiled as he looked around; they were standing behind a fairly big crowd. A gathering like the metal concerts he loved to go to. Only this crowd was much more diverse and less intimidating: old and young, rich and – apparently – poor. Men in suits and ties, men with long beards wearing leather jackets, women in high heels carrying expensive bags, and girls in ripped t-shirts. People of every skin color, ethnicity and build. After everything he'd been through, William thought it was silly to categorize people by their appearance, if not deplorable in the first place.

"Where are we this time, Milena?" he asked.

"This, William, is ground zero for the biggest milestone on the road to the new world order. It's three years after where I picked you up. More accurately, *when* I picked you up. It's 2025. Here, you will be giving your most controversial but also the most inspiring speech. This is where the bonfire is lit," Milena replied.

"Speech? Me? Oh, no, no… I have stage fright, I

stutter even when I talk in front of a few people. I thought I was supposed to write a book or something and others would pick it up from there," said William. He looked stressed, even though it wasn't really him who was about to talk in front of hundreds of people.

"You did write a book, William. And it resonated in the hearts and minds of many. They listened to your ideas at book signing events, which led to casual indoor meetings until it reached the point where you had to put speakers out for people eager to hear your ideas. Eventually, the only places that could take your audience was outdoor arenas. This is your biggest crowd yet: over seven hundred. Don't forget, every second is also broadcast live. Your speech will reach thousands, maybe more than a hundred thousand. For a guy who wrote a book on social problems and offered solutions, which the majority of mainstream media and critics called fantastical and childish, this is really impressive. Your words were not new to them. It was what you offered as a solution that got the attention of the masses, the people fed up with things. And the way you present your ideas, oh, how you fired them up."

"Well, I really would love to see myself do it. No way I'll believe it otherwise," He smiled. "Can anyone see us?"

"No, they can't. We can roam around freely. We are like ghosts here. Enjoy!"

"Let's move in closer then. I want to hear what they're saying," said William. They joined the crowd from the middle of the rear row. William led, wanting to take in everyone; so he walked all the way to the right before turning to walk all the way left, like a scanner. The crowd was even more varied than it originally looked. He had never seen so many different people together in one place. It looked like a gathering of a vast variety of world views, which in any other situation could well have ended in fisticuffs. Preachers were talking to rabbis as imams chatted to … tough guys?

How the hell did I manage to get them all together? he thought.

"Don't answer that!" William quipped.

"I wasn't going to," she joked back.

William's glance fell on someone he used to know. A vagabond he used to see on the way home, someone he gave coffee and a sandwich every day for nearly a year. At times they talked for a bit. The guy said he had not always been this way; he'd been doing fine until 2008. The year the worst economic crisis hit the world. William always found it easy to talk to him. He enjoyed their chats to some degree, although they did feel like unpleasant tales. He remembered thinking, *This guy seems healthy enough; why can't he find a job and work like normal people?* His charity was more self-justification – he was rich and had a higher status – than sincere interest. He was doing the right thing and interacting with the common man, that was all. On one occasion, the vagabond mentioned a sick son; the government wouldn't cover the expensive treatment needed and he was terrified of losing the boy. "One good thing I did in this shitty world," he'd said. *Sure hope he doesn't take it the wrong way and ask for money,* William remembered thinking at the time.

What was his name, something like Jake or Jack? Jacob! Yes, it was Jacob. Jacob. What a hopeful name for a guy who begged for a living.

Jacob was now among the people who came to listen to his future self. He still looked like a vagabond. William looked him in the eye, only to realize that Jacob couldn't see him. He put his arm on Jacob's shoulder. It fell through the man, like a hologram. He wanted to say hi and ask how Jacob's son was, sincerely this time.

As they continued to wander through the crowd, he started to focus on what people were talking about.

"This guy used to be very rich, you know. Then he sold his company and all his assets and gave the money to his employees, provided they sent their kids to the school he founded. It's free and they teach good manners. He's no fraud; he's the real deal."

"His book changed my life. I feel like I found words for my inner screams of revolt. He is truly gifted. This is the third time I'm listening to him; I discover something new each time."

"First time I saw him was on the internet. I thought he was preaching total nonsense. But my wife insisted on taking me to a meeting. I actually got in a heated argument with him even to a point of insulting him. He was more than understanding and offered to chat one on one after the meeting. That talk changed my mind. I read his book and kept in touch. He really has a way of convincing people."

"What a sham; I'm only here because my brother is into this guy and forced me to come."

"The visions he claims to have seen, as inspiring as they sound, are just marketing tools for his book. It seems they work though. – Why am I here, then? Not sure, to be honest. He puts on a great show and for some reason, I'm intrigued to hear what he has to offer. One thing we agree on is that this world is fucked up, intolerably so."

"I read his book and was hooked on his storytelling. His arguments are spot on. And the best bit? He has a formula to change things. Probably not feasible yet, though."

"This is no conspiracy theory, man, there is an evil cabal ruling over us. Can't you see the state the world is in? Everyone's unhappy and miserable. We all live like slaves to money and products. Hell, people around the world, children for God's sake, die in wars for oil. The world is on the brink of social and economic collapse, we can't go on like this forever, someone needs to raise their voice to the evil overlords."

"His views on organized religion and royalty mirror my own. The monarchs and religious leaders use fear and terror to oppress humankind. Why the hell should people give their hard-earned money to so-called royals whose only qualification is to be the offspring of a long gone king or queen? I mean, the right people sleep together and boom, you're born with a silver spoon. Well, ninety-nine percent of us are not so lucky with our parents' sex life; we come into this world with a wooden stake up our asses and struggle to survive by clawing our way forward. Where is the justice in this? Where are those so-called fundamental human rights? If you're born rich, you live like every day is a party. If you're born poor, you count the days till you die. I'm telling you; these monarchs and those religious leaders must be put to rest already. They are the parasites of this world."

"I like this guy," William said.

"He is not alone, you know?" Milena replied.

"The main aspects of his argument contradict his past. He may have forsaken his way of life but this doesn't make him an honest man. How much money and fame do you think he earns from this charade, can you imagine? No, Mister, I have seen your kind before; you will be exposed sooner or later."

"Not this one, though," William said smiling.

"Give them a chance, William. They have been disappointed by frauds and hypocrites for so long," Milena answered.

"This man may not have said it yet. But he is clearly grooming people for a cult where he will declare himself a messiah. This is blasphemy. I'm here to protest him and report him to the authorities as a good citizen and a responsible clergyman."

William was quite calm as listened to it all. He was surprised to find himself unaffected by the praise or the scorn; he had a newfound unselfishness and tolerance. He realized he had ripped off his skin of ego.

On reaching the other end of the crowd, nearer the podium, he saw familiar faces beside the lectern where his near-future self was about to give his biggest and most controversial speech yet. Seated silently on plastic chairs, Rachel, Charlie and Candice were looking around curiously.

"God, I missed them so much; it feels like I've not seen them for months, even though I did just this morning. How strange…" sighed William.

"They'll be waiting for you when we get back soon, William."

"Rachel doesn't look all that keen."

"She's having a hard time coping with your sudden popularity and your new way of living. She's also a little worried about your wellbeing, William. It's only natural. As a mother and a wife who has dedicated her life to her family, it has been difficult to adjust to your battle against everything she had gratefully accepted since birth. Your war with the status quo doesn't make as much sense to her. She lost many friends and comforts along the way. Despite her reluctance, however, she supported you no matter what," Milena said.

"I see. I hope one day she understands. Rachel is the best mother and companion anyone can hope for. I always considered myself blessed to have her. And never could figure out what I'd done to deserve someone like that."

"Don't sell yourself short, William. Kindred souls tend to find each other. Your differences complement each other," Milena replied, "Oh, I think it's time. Look at all the fuss up there."

William looked up at the podium. People were rushing around to check the electronic equipment. Not that there was much. The whole set-up consisted of a big screen and a single microphone. That was all. This had to be the final sound and vision check then, before his future self took the stage.

And then, the cheering came like a thundering roar. It wasn't every day someone could see himself from another one's perspective.

Future William appeared in front of the cheap-looking curtain and slowly walked towards the lectern. His hands were folded in gratitude. Diffident as he looked, there was determination in his eyes too. Without further ado, he started to speak.

"Welcome my fellow humans; it is an honor to stand in front of you all."

Cheering carried on, still roaring, except for a small, yet undeniable number of stern faces, hands refusing to applaud and arms crossed tight.

"Look around, look around," he nodded, "I see many familiar faces; faces I have come to call friends. And I see lots of fresh ones too. I sincerely welcome you all. Either you are here out of curiosity, real interest, or to see the enemy closer.

"My name is William Rudned. I'm neither a politician nor a leader of any kind. I have no plans to be one. I'm just someone who has seen and lived through certain things and come to the conclusion that the world we are living in is a man-made hell, that we are not free: we are the slaves of the over-demons who shape and rule the world using mechanisms we have all accepted as norms. I wrote a book about what I learned in the hope of pointing out to my fellow humans who were stuck in a loop most of their lives and knew deep inside, that a better way was possible. I have witnessed that better way and put the formula on the table for everyone to see. In spite of all the rejections, humiliations and ridicule, I stand by it. From the looks of it, I'm not alone. This gives me the courage and strength to carry on with my fight against these over-demons and crush their insidious design once and for all. So I want each and every one of you to take a moment to congratulate yourselves for your bravery to join my struggle. Applaud not me but your own selves; you deserve it."

The echo of hundreds of cheers reached three blocks away.

"Now let's get on with it," resumed future William, "Since the dawn of history, humankind has advanced in every aspect of life. In science, political systems, arts, music, social order, and many more aspects of modern society. We have seen empires rise and fall, kings and queens come and go, we have seen heroes, villains, beliefs and wars. We have erected new towers of Babel, built astonishing buildings, discovered some of the secrets of nature and cosmos, sent people to space and the moon. We have come so far as a civilization that one would be forgiven for thinking the outcome would be fantastic for all mankind. But can any one of you claim to be happy and satisfied with your lives? Can you take a step back, look at yourself and say that you prospered and advanced to reach your potential as an intelligent being whose biggest feat is personal improvement?" he asked, eyes blazing.

"No!" came a fierce roar from the majority of the crowd.

"And tell me: can we honestly claim human rights exist if they are not applied fairly to all? It's the year 2025 and there are still people, children dying of poverty and hunger all over the world, while others have the means to feed their babies on exclusive formulas. Where is the justice in this? What happened to human rights? Are some considered humans while others are labeled as a sub-species? We need to stop persuading ourselves that there is such a thing as human rights in this world. It is an illusion; a comforting lie we pretend to believe to relieve ourselves of the responsibilities we have as human beings. The bosom of the world is big enough to feed everyone. Yet, a minority of endlessly greedy powerholders usurp that bounty and grow fat, while others perish watching them feast. Should we accept this situation as the way it is?"

"No!" A louder and angrier roar reached well beyond the earlier three blocks.

"So I ask you: who are these powers that are holding us back? Who deprives us of the most fundamental right to life?"

"The over-demons!" clamored the crowd in unison.

"And who are they?" William asked again.

A plethora of names came from the crowd.

"That's right! The holier-than-thou religious leaders, the greedy money brokers, the oil barons, the vile media, the self-serving and oppressive high-tech moguls, the parasite kings and queens, the exploitative legions of tyrants!"

He paused to catch his breath. A punishing schedule of speeches over many months had taken their toll on his health, especially on his voice and breath.

"The world has become a marketplace of flesh and ego, and the currency is our souls. We, during our journey from the caves to our metropolises, have slowly but surely turned into aimless consumers. The thesis with money and domination in its foundation, the system that has risen on the shoulders of the people, the order of the world that was formed hundreds of years ago, no longer works. Not that it ever did in the first place. Its faults were noted by many great men, whose solutions were to create the antithesis of the current one. But what they never took into account was, if one is corruptible, so is its opposite. And we have seen them fall too. What we need is not one edge or the other but the sweet spot of balance. What we need is a synthesis! Today, I will tell you about this synthesis, as I have witnessed it firsthand!"

A chorus of whistles and applause rose as the air was charged with electricity.

"I have seen a world of joy, peace, prosperity, justice, and harmony! A world free of oppression, free of evil and dishonest governments, free of the tyranny of holy men and money lenders. A world where people live not to surpass one another in beauty and wealth but in their contribution to their environment and their gains in knowledge, in their struggle to reach their full potential as divine beings. A world where people create to enhance their souls and mind and consume only if needed. This, my friends, is not a dream but a possibility waiting for you to grasp.

"In that world, every newborn is molded in the pot of righteousness, honesty, ethics, compassion, love and respect. No individual is deprived of this most fundamental right, the right education. There is no money because everything belongs to the people as a whole. What you pay for now, what we wage war for today, what we kill babies for; energy, technology, housing, food, and every natural resource are free there. Technology works for people, not the other way around. Everyone has equal rights and equal opportunities. People of that world are free in every way we are not. They love life, seeing it as a miracle and a gift, not despising it as we do. Because they matter, what they do matters, everything about their lives is worth getting up for every day, with hope and appetite for what the new day's sun may bring. No one's loved ones suffer illnesses because they are poor, for health services are free to all and comprehensive."

As future William said these last words, he caught sight of Jacob. As if he already knew Jacob was there and even precisely where he stood. He gazed at that tense face and nodded. Jacob responded with a little half smile, looking uncomfortable than surprised.

"They are ruled by wise men, who hold the people above their selfish impulses, by virtue and honor. Wise men, elected by enlightened and conscious people, not by their false promises, fake smiles and their severe propaganda but with their proven characters and their worthy actions."

"What about God?!" someone from the crowd called out.

"What about it?" William shouted back.

"Where is God in all this? Did you kill him too?" asked the same man.

"I killed no one and no one killed God. They just evolved. And for God, he is there too, as he has always been, unknown but endlessly sought, unseen but imagined, not present but depended on. God, my friend, has just changed form there. It is the supreme force of anything and everything, directly connected to anyone willing to make contact. Not a fearful deity, contactable only by the mediation of self-appointed agents. God there is everywhere and easily accessible, my friend," he answered calmly. There was no reply.

"No one disputes anyone's belief there. Everyone is free to believe and practice anything. No judgments, no persecution. Freedom and respect are embedded in one's core. A person's only individual mantra is not to impose anything unwelcome on others. This is the golden rule of every intelligent being. Collective good above individual desire is glorified. These are the water and sun of that harmonious world." Bewildered faces stared at him.

"I know what I preach doesn't make much sense to you now. I don't blame you. How could it, when harmony and compassion are just fancy words you've never seen in action? When clemency, love and respect are considered ancient virtues long gone, in a world that rewards cruelty, greed and hubris?

"Life is really simple, my friends. It is we who insist on making it complicated. We allow those in power to trap us in our egos, in our narcissism and selfishness…" he said and paused, eyes clouding as he looked down, "We allow them keep us ignorant, base and selfish, we let them drug us with trivial subjects and unnecessary materialistic desires; the result is masses who'll accept anything without question, as long as it is repeated often and loud enough. We let them limit our mindset, possess us with fear. This is our biggest sin. A sin we commit against our souls and minds."

A silence fell upon the crowd. Then he raised his head, looking stern, eyes blazing with fury. His posture resembled a ticking bomb that was about to explode. The face on the big screen galvanized the crowd.

"This is their control mechanism. And it is bound to get only worse if we do not unchain our minds right now, no later. We, my friends, have been wallowing in shallow waters, fascinated by the variety of pebbles. It is the deep waters of a vast ocean where we will find endless lifeforms and miracles of all kinds. We must venture into the ocean to see what has been kept secret from us. But we must first learn how to swim, which takes knowledge and wisdom to gather the necessary skills. Then, and only then, will the doors of that paradise open for us. If we want to reach that paradise, we must be vigilant. We must wake up. The world is terminally ill and the only cure is our resolve to live the way we were supposed to. In connection with nature, with our souls and with the universe. United under the banner of righteousness, morality and respect. We must cut out the cancer that has been polluting our souls, our minds and our planet. The parasitic kings and queens, the pompous royals and dynasties, the sycophantic media moguls, the tyrannical and hypocritical politicians, the dictators and warlords, the self-righteous popes and sheiks, the smug big tech tycoons, the evil oil barons and the greedy bankers, the crime lords, and every other participant forming and enabling this cabal must go. Mankind has been their slaves and steppingstones for far too long. We have been kept busy with trivialities so we won't protest. We have been zombified with social media so we stay numb. We have been thrown into this vicious circle of working nine to five, for the sole purpose of needlessly and endlessly earning money and consuming, just to satisfy a never-ending hunger for material goods, so that we fail to see the truth, that we, the people hold the real power. And worst of all, we accept this as natural. Don't give in to their unfounded doctrine of misguided democracy or morals. Without knowledge, wisdom or righteousness, democracy is bound to lack justice, providence and most importantly, freedom. These institutions and their corrupt representatives must be buried deep into history so that a new and better human civilization can arise. A new era cannot be built into the old system but must blossom upon the ashes of it. The surgical blade of the people must cut out these diseased cells once and for all. Money must go, organized religion institutions must go, the evil over-lords must go. The oasis of a new world is just a jump ahead. Equality, justice, happiness are only a reach away, waiting for us to seize them. Humankind, awake! Stand up to your unseen masters. Break down the walls erected in your minds, find your true self, the one that shines. Humankind, awake and take your rightful place in the Cosmos!" panted future William, covered in sweat.

"He is swimming in dangerous waters…" a slightly worried present William said. It was awkward, referring to himself in the third person.

"Isn't he right, though?"

"You know what I think. This doesn't change the fact that he's treading on powerful toes and he is very hostile. This is not like me. Is this the only possible outcome for me? Will I inevitably be this harsh and radical?"

"Everything is fluid, William. Only you will determine your future, no one else. Nothing is inevitable," said Milena.

"Look at Rachel; she looks worried too. Certainly not happy with the way this is progressing. Have all my speeches been this fierce?"

"No, I told you, this one is special. It is the biggest milestone in what you started. After today, nothing will be the same again. Look at the crowd, William, look at the glow in their eyes, look at their chins lifting up."

As future William continued his speech, Jacob's eyes began to fill. No drop had fallen yet but his eyelids and lips were shaking like leaves in a stiff wind, trying to hold on to their branch to avoid being scattered into the unknown. He looked full of intense emotions, ready to erupt at any moment.

Future William stopped. Wiped the sweat off his forehead. Closing his eyes briefly, he gave a long sigh. He then turned back to his roaring crowd and spoke calmly:

"One who sells weapons does not want peace. One who sells medicine does not want health. One who sells belief does not want knowledge. And more than anything, they want us to stay as individuals because they know they'd be powerless, unable to keep us down if we're united. They want us to stay ignorant and numb because they know we would see them as they are if we're awake: evil and malicious. They are the minority; *we* are the majority. They may pay for their security with a benevolent police force – who are not all corrupt; most share the same misfortunes that befall us. We just have to find the courage to say *no more*! We must leave our selfness behind in favor of our collective might. We must leave behind our ego and ignorance so that we join in consciousness and attain our divinity. This is my wish for us. This is my testament to you."

The crowd's response was phenomenal. Everyone was fired up and united in their misery, like a hive, shouting together:

"Awake, arise, awake, arise!"

For a minute, the man on the stage closed his eyes and listened reverently to the roaring crowd. Opening his eyes again, he rolled his sleeve and glanced at his watch.

Right then, a man in the crowd raised his smartphone to video the speech. Present William, standing behind him caught sight of the time on the phone. It was 7.43 p.m.

Future William had just looked at his own watch. With a glance at the crowd and a deep sigh, he slowly turned his head back for a look at his family. His beloved wife and most precious beings. The fire in his eyes had given way to concern and tenderness. Charlie and Candice looked bored. He gazed at them for a while, his sad face glowing, as if taking a mental picture. The children didn't take notice but Rachel saw it. There was something in there. Something he had been hiding. Something terrible.

Gazing at his wife, future William mouthed *I love you*.

Rachel was perturbed. This wasn't the time. *What on earth brought it on now?* she thought, feeling the uneasiness spread.

Then he turned his head to Jacob, gave him a forgiving look and whispered:

"It's OK."

"I'm sorry!" Jacob yelled, "I must. I don't have a choice. For my son!"

Two teardrops ran softly down his cheeks.

A scream came from the crowd:

"He's got a gun!"

A loud bang.

"Oh my God, William!" Rachel yelled, running toward her husband.

Chaos erupted as panicked yells filled the air.

Kneeling down beside William bleeding motionless on the floor, Rachel covered his body with hers.

"Somebody, call an ambulance!" she screamed and turned to her children. They were frozen solid in shock and terror, "Get back behind the stage. Stay there. Do not come out!"

"Oh, no! Why, why didn't you tell me?" a desolate present William shouted at Milena.

"Because William, first you must see *what* could be. What you could lead to," Milena said. There was no regret in her voice, only sorrow. "This is what is necessary for your message to be heard by millions, William. This is your sacrifice for the future that might be."

It was pandemonium. William tried to see his future self but there was too much commotion around the stage.

"Why is it necessary? Isn't the message clear enough? Why should this happen to me to be heard?" came his panicked question.

"People rarely value words, William; they hear them, approve of them, may even be moved by them, but eventually, they forget every word. Only through trauma do people tend to remember and feel them from the heart."

"But why would they bother to assassinate me? I could only gather a few hundred people; I'm not that big a threat to them!"

"You're not now but you have the potential to be. It would have been much more noticeable if they had eliminated you after you had reached much wider audiences. This method has worked for them perfectly before, countless times. But this time, it will backfire." Milena then revealed the prophecy. "Your assassination here will echo throughout the world. The exact opposite of what they intended will happen. People will take notice. They will question why you were assassinated. Who shot you and why? Who they used to do it, and how they exploited him? Then a year later, a young boy you've never met will read your story. He will be deeply affected by it. He will study your book, he will improve it, deepen its core message and create a new hypothesis. He will grow up to inspire others and begin to unite them under your principles. That boy will lay down the bricks on the road to the future you have visited. But that boy will only hear about you because of the events that have unfolded here."

William looked at the podium again, hoping to see his future self. He still couldn't see where he lay, where he was shot, or how bad it was. Then a gap opened between all those bodies for a split second. He realized his future self was looking directly at him.

"Milena, I saw him; he was looking at me, can he see me?" he asked tensely.

"Yes, he can. You see, he was right where you were, seen what you have seen. He has been aware of our presence all along," Milena replied, "Would you like to say goodbye?"

"Goodbye? Oh my God, I really am going to die here, aren't I?" William asked, frightened and desperate.

"Yes, I'm afraid you are," she answered without looking at him.

His heart started to pound as it never had. Not like anything he had before; it was somewhat different. Pounding without fear or terror, yet desolate. How could anyone say farewell to their own selves? How could someone bear witness to their own death?

"He would like that, you know," she added.

"I don't know what to say," William sniffled.

"You don't have to say anything. Everything that's worth saying had already been said."

William wandered around aimlessly to calm down, to face reality. Jacob was taken down to the ground by several officers and handcuffed behind the back; he was bawling his eyes out and repenting loudly all the while.

"God, forgive me, oh God, forgive me, they made me, I had no choice, they made me, oh dear lord!"

William pitied him, finding kindness in his heart for the man who had shot him, even at that moment. Anger and hate seemed to have no power over him.

He turned back to the podium; the crowd had been dispersed by the police. The man lying in a pool of his own blood was surrounded by a group of officers. Right that moment, his eyes locked with those of his future self. There was a kind of peace blended with a mild fear in his doppelgänger's eyes. Eyes beckoning him. He knew he had to do it, even if it would be painful beyond imagination.

"Yes, I want to say goodbye... Oh, God, help me..." said William.

They climbed onto the stage to approach the man lying down next to the lectern, bleeding and white as paper, but apparently at peace. He turned his eyes toward them without moving his head and smiled. Blood covered his teeth.

"Hi, Milena, long time no see..." he managed a whisper.

"Hey, William... It's almost over, Pups. I'm so proud of the man you have become," she said.

"Yeah, we've come a long way, you and I, right?" William said, "Will I ever see you again?"

"Anything is possible, Pups..."

"William, hang on, help is on the way, stay with me,

William, I love you…" Rachel spoke to her husband. It was too noisy for her to hear him or ask whom he was talking to.

"Hey handsome, what's with the long face?" the bleeding man asked his past self.

William couldn't find anything to say back. He was barely able to speak. All he could do was give a wry, tearful smile through trembling lips.

"Don't worry, I have no regrets, I made my peace a long time ago. Dying is a small price to pay for a future worth living for," said future William.

"You're not going to die, do you hear me, you will live, you will stay with us, we'll grow old together! Do you hear me!" Rachel said, thinking he was talking to her.

"Milena, you know I always wanted to kiss you, right?" the dying man asked.

"You know I do," Milena said with a gentle smile. Lowering her head, she placed her lips on the trembling mouth and gave him a long kiss. Rachel saw the strange movement of her husband's lips but was too terrified to ascribe a meaning to it.

"Just the way I imagined it would feel," future William said with a grin.

He looked up at the clear sky; it was nearly night and the stars were beginning to shine. Barely moving his mouth, he said:

"Beautiful…"

And gave one last long breath.

Rachel felt its warmth on her face.

"No, no, no! William, please come back, don't leave me yet, please William, I can't…" she burst into tears before completing her sentence.

"Goodbye, Pups, Godspeed," said Milena.

William was still weeping when she placed her right hand on his left shoulder. The light flashed again in front of his eyes for the last time.

CHAPTER 6
TUUM ARBITRIUM

The cigar smoldered on the bench. The thickness of smoke indicated that it had been no more than a few minutes since was lit, perhaps even less.

A cat sat next to one of legs of the bench, whiskers twitching curiously at the acrid smell. It jumped twice its height when two people popped out of thin air. One of them nearly stepped on it. Alarmed, the cat hissed and ran away. This was clearly not its night.

The man with eyes red as the morning sun sat down on the bench and put his head between his knees. The woman sat upright beside him and rubbed his back. Lifting his head, he placed it on her lap, clung to her and burst into distraught tears.

"Let it all out, Pups, after all, you are only human," she said.

He carried on shaking with sobs, choking.

"It is the only way, William," said Milena softly, sleek yet firm fingers stroking his hair. Every second about this moment felt like a déjà vu for William.

"Sometimes, the wheels of fate don't turn without blood to oil the shafts, William," she continued, "As it was before, so it is now."

Every time she spoke, he clung to her harder.

"But you do have a choice," she said, continuing to stroke his hair. It wasn't the first time she had lied about her caress, nor would it be the last.

"You can choose to forget everything you've been through and carry on as you are. You'll have an honest life, a decent life. You'll succeed at work and add value to the lives of the people around you. You'll be happy most of the time and sad only on occasion. But overall, it will be a good life. And you will have a long life; you'll be rich. You'll see your children grow up to be good people, you will see them fall in love and marry. You'll be there when their children come into the world. You'll hug your grandchildren with your wife beside you. You'll see them grow too. They will adore you and seek guidance from you. You will give your children and their children after them everything you were deprived of as a child. Seeing their happiness will cure your broken heart, until your past misery will only be a distant memory, an unpleasant dream. You will have much to celebrate and enjoy the warmth of a family. As you get older, you will be proud of what you've accomplished and the reputation you will leave behind. And when it is your time, you will die. All your family will mourn your loss. So will your friends. Your passing will leave a void in a lot of people's hearts. They will remember you, share their memories with one another, sometimes they will laugh, sometimes they will cry. But like everything, it will fade with time and one day, you will be a picture on a piano your descendants rarely stop and look. The world will continue to spin, good will be good, bad will stay bad and so it will go on as long as it will."

"But nothing will change, isn't that right? The world will continue to be a shitty place and people will continue to suffer and die for no good reason, under the boots of a few elite evil men?" asked William, still crying on Milena's lap.

"Yes, William, you're right," she said, her hands now on his cheeks.

William sat up, wiped his sticky wet face with his coat sleeve, looked straight at the beautiful woman with yellow eyes and said:

"You can't put this on my shoulders... Why is it my responsibility to start a revolution – by dying an awful death in front of my family? Why should it be me, huh? Why not someone else? Someone else with nothing to lose?"

"There is no *why* here, William. It just *is*," replied Milena, "The universe has aligned fate in this direction. The whys are not relevant. What is important is the choice that will be made. I'm not saying it is fair, it is not. But fairness has nothing to do with this, neither does the reason behind your appointment to this position. The only thing that matters here is the choice. Will it be this or that, will you stay or go, will you do it or will you not... Nothing else is of any significance. Fate does not care about your hesitation or your inner struggle. It does not care if you have everything to lose. It only cares about your choice."

"Fuck fate! I have children, I have responsibilities! They need me to raise them right, they need my guidance, my support. Did fate take this into account, huh? I determine my own fate, no one else! Not God, not you, not anyone, do you understand me?" William exploded.

"I do, William and I sympathize with you, believe me. But the higher power doesn't deal with detail, only in decisions. Fate is the agent of the higher power and it's constantly fluid. It changes depending on the choices you make. So you have a choice. You determine your own fate."

"I thought fate was certain. Predetermined, immutable."

"No, Pups, this is one of the fabrications of your religions, to manipulate you into believing you are bound by what your god, or in their case, what *they*, say will and has to happen. It is one of the mechanisms of keeping you in check," Milena explained, "Fate is everchanging; everything is possible at once. Every choice you make alters the course of what will happen. The chain of events coming after a significant choice is what is called *fate*. The only fate that is absolute is what we make for ourselves."

William sat up taller and turned towards the lake. It was a clear night; moonlight bathed the still surface of the water. It was a lovely scene. Shimmering waters waltzing with the moon. A view he had looked at hundreds of times before. But at that moment, he realized he was seeing it for the first time.

"How we take everything for granted..." he whispered.

"Because you're preoccupied with minutiae that you should never waste time on," she replied, "And you forget death is but a hair's breadth away."

William kept looking into the distance as Milena carried on.

"There is one more thing we need to cover before you decide."

"I've had it, Milena; I can't take any more of this," said William still gazing at the beautiful lake.

"I'm sorry, but we have to. We have a missing part of the equation," Milena replied, "We have understood the enemy, broke it into pieces and assembled the whole structure again. We know them now... But we still don't know you."

"Haven't we already talked about me?"

"We did, Pups. But you are not the same man who started this journey. You have changed. You have evolved. When you embarked on this journey, you were confused and dazed, living through life aimlessly, seeking a higher meaning and reason for everything that exists, including yourself. But now, after everything you have experienced, you see in more colors than anyone else alive."

"I can't see anything. I've gone blind!"

"It's only natural to think this way; you need time to absorb it all, put it all together in order to use your heightened senses and wisdom so you can look down from above and see what has reformed," Milena said.

"I don't know who I am anymore, Milena. In fact, I never did and maybe never will."

"Let me help you to figure it out, then," she said soothingly, "After all, that is *my* purpose."

"Let me give you the bad news: you've most probably failed in fulfilling your purpose," said William regretfully.

"That's precisely what we have to tackle William: your lack of faith in yourself. You, Pups, have one of the brightest lights I have seen in anyone. But you've been conditioned to hide it, block it all your life. You were brainwashed into believing that your inner light is not what the world needs, that you are not special or worthy. That is and always has been your blue pill. Spit it out now and see yourself as you are; a beautiful, powerful and self-reliant lifeforce."

"Lifeforce, eh? I'm not even sure what life is, let alone be a force of it. What if I can't see what you do?" he objected.

"There is no *can* or *cannot*, William; there is only the choice: *to do* or *not to do*. Remember when you were pure? Before you were crushed by your parents under the responsibilities of everyday life? Go back to your roots. Find William Version 1.0. How was it then?"

William's mind went blank for a moment. What was his original self like? Before he was contaminated with fear and hate? He tried to remember some of the songs he used to listen to then; that was the way his memory worked. One song popped into his mind:

Oh, I get hysterical, hysteria
When you get that feelin', do you believe it?
It's such a magical mysteria
When you get that feelin', better start believing
'Cause it's a miracle, I see you will, ooh babe
Hysteria when you're near

The memory brought up two words:

"Hopeful… ecstatic…" whispered William.

"And, what else? Tell me all of it. Remember, William, you must remember."

"Joyful. I was happy, full of dreams, full of ambition and heart."

"Go on, deep diver, I want it all," Milena pressed.

"I wanted to change the world. Make it a better place. I wanted to be happy and make others happy. I dreamt of glory, honor, justice, and divinity. I wanted to see the unseen, know the unknown. I wanted to learn all the secrets of the world. I wanted to rise above my bodily self and be one with something higher, more divine. I wanted every day to be an adventure. I wanted to speak my mind… I wanted to create things."

"What did you want to create?" Milena asked.

"I don't know. Something truly meaningful. Something that will add value to life. Not a device or something material but an idea, an idea powerful enough to spread through humankind like wildfire and destroy monsters. I wanted to ascend above myself and take everyone with me…" said William, "I remember its heat, the flames of the fire within me covering my body; it was like all my nerve endings were little people yelling war cries, challenging the world, beating their chests. But that was a child's dream, a product of the fairy tales of heroes long forgotten; nothing more."

"No, it was not, William. Those dreams and urges were there for a reason. The very reason you seek. The reason for your existence. That is why even your body was reacting. It was put there by something, something that has its own mind and plans. Nothing was a coincidence or a dream but an echo of the fate that you can create. Now you have the chance to realize it."

"But I no longer feel the same. That purity was consumed by hate and fear," said William.

"Maybe not. Maybe it has just been overshadowed by them."

"I don't know. The only thing I know is when I think of my childhood, all I recall is the darkness,"

"Tell me about it," Milena said.

"Why? So I can present myself as a victim of my parents?"

"But you are, aren't you? There is nothing to be ashamed in being a victim, William. They should be ashamed of themselves for what they'd done to you. Tell me, please…"

"I… I don't want to."

"You have to face them, William. You have to confront your fears and get over your traumas."

"What: should I forgive them?"

"It is your choice. Forgive them, judge them, curse them. But don't bury your misery. You must cut it like the Gordian knot it is. Otherwise, it will always feed on you."

William kept quiet for a while. The warm smile on his face was all but lost now.

"Don't frown!" shouted his father's memory.

"God, I hate you, you heartless son of a bitch! How could you be so cruel! I loved you… All I wanted was to be like you…" William yelled like there was someone facing him, "What was so bad about me that you hated me so much? What have I ever done to you?"

"Maybe he was trying to toughen you in his own way?" Milena asked.

"Fuck that! He was pure evil. He enjoyed taking it out on me. I was his whipping boy. All I needed was just a smidgen of love. And some guidance. But no, he gave me the exact opposite. He made me feel like shit!"

"You'd have to be a psychopath to wear that!" his father had said about his Iron Maiden t-shirt with *Trooper Eddie* on it.

"He loathed me. He wished I wasn't his son. He never found me worthy."

"What did it mean to be worthy?" asked Milena.

"I was never successful in school as he was or in business. I was never fearless in life as he wanted me to be."

"And you accepted this as the condition for being worthy? Is life all about success in business or the ability to earn money? Did you ever care about these things in the first place?"

"I thought I did. I longed to become a successful businessman for a time. But I never made it. After a while, I stopped caring altogether. Maybe it was my way of protecting myself by considering it meaningless. You know how the subconscious works. We're capable of convincing ourselves of just about anything, as long as it suits us. I may have done the same thing about being successful. If I couldn't achieve it, then I could at least persuade myself that it didn't really matter that much."

"Did you ever consider that you really didn't care about earning money or success in business? You may not have tasted it but you could have known that life was much more than business, that being worthy of something or for someone is just a cruel conception?"

"I don't understand what you're trying to explain, Milena," said William, confused.

"What I mean is that being worthy has nothing to do with other people. You're the one who should decide if you are worthy of something. Not your father, not society.

And being rich or successful in a crooked business world as it is today has nothing to do with being worthy. On the contrary, most of those so-called successful people are not even worthy of being loved. The majority of them are total scumbags."

"Perhaps. But this doesn't change the fact that whatever I do, how pleasant and kind I try to be, even as a husband or a father, I never feel like I'm worthy. Not worthy of love, not worthy of happiness, not even worthy of living… I just can't," he said dejectedly.

"But you are, William. You were always special. You even had visions, didn't you?"

"Visions?" he asked, surprised, trying to remember what she meant. Then it came to him. "Oh, yes… I did, once. I haven't thought about them for a long time… "

"You had instant and powerful visions of near-future events."

"Yes, but they didn't last. I lost them when I was around fourteen."

"Did you ever think about why, William?"

"I did. Never figured it out, though. One day, they just left and never came back."

"Think harder. There must be something that caused it. Did you ever share them with anyone?"

"Yes… I did. With my father. After the third one. It was a big one. I remember I nearly fainted when the vision came. I was with my friends in a ski lounge, sitting by the fire at night. When it happened, I put my head between my legs, so that they wouldn't see my catatonic face. I just told them I had a terrible migraine and left. In that image, I saw the death of a politician in a traffic accident with his whole family three days before it actually happened. The previous ones were not that significant. But that one was so lucid that when it came true, I had to share it with someone or I'd have lost my mind. I was scared. None of my friends would have taken me seriously – or worse, they'd have made fun of me. So I decided to tell my father, not that I got my hopes up. But I needed him to help me understand what was going on."

"How did he react?" Milena asked.

"Giving me a downcast look, he asked, 'William, do we have to call Doctor Meinheimer again?' It would've been less painful if he'd just made fun of me. He treated me like a nutcase. He never took me seriously after that."

"What about your mother? You never talk about her. Why is that?"

"My mother was a ghost. A weak woman lost in her own hell, living with an abusive monster. She was always absent. It was not that she was a bad person, she was just not there. She never stood up for herself or me. Actually, I always considered myself an orphan, even when both my parents were alive."

"I see. So after your father's typical approach to your incident, you blocked your senses, your gift, just because a narrow-minded man couldn't even see the possibility of possessing senses other than touch, smell or hearing."

"It's possible," said William regretfully.

"That was a gift only special ones are blessed with. You also had the gift of will. Do you remember it?"

"What is the gift of will? I don't remember anything other than those brief visions."

"Oh, but you do know and remember it... You just named it wrongly," said Milena.

"What do you mean?"

"You thought it was the answer to your prayers to God. Do you remember the time you prayed with all your heart for a girl? When you were around fifteen? You fell in love, and you prayed for her to love you back," Milena replied.

"I... I think I do. Holy shit, what was her name?" William wondered.

"Leslie Howler," answered Milena with a smile.

"Yes, Leslie... Oh my God! I haven't thought of her for thirty years. I remember now. I remember how I prayed, holding my hands up," said William.

"That was not God's blessing to you. Not in a sense you think it was, anyway. It was you. Your gift of will made it a reality. Your pure intention made it a reality. That is a gift still embedded in you. It was never lost. Trust me. It stays dormant inside you. Once you cleanse your soul, it will surface again. In fact, every one of you has that power within you. But only some of you are spiritually developed enough to harness it without training. You are one of them, William. Not were, are," Milena said encouragingly, "The important thing to understand is that your father, the successful larger-than-life figure, saw that light and was envious. He was so egotistical and unsure of himself that he always wanted to keep you down so that you can never rise higher than him. He was weak and pathetic. Not someone powerful like you imagined. Let him fade away. He can't hurt you anymore," said Milena, warming his heart, and continued, "You, my dear William, were meant to have Daniel Rudned as your father. Everyone has a purpose in life. No one exists without reason. His reason for existence was to torment you so that you can be who you are now. All that hate and fear led you to withdraw from the material world, to question the deeper aspects of life. Your gifts seemed lost to you but all that pain you endured sharpened them; they are more powerful than ever now. You, Pups, are the perfect creature born out of darkness to seek out and amplify the light like no one has ever done before. Greatness always blossoms under the immense pressure of agony. Let go of him now; his purpose is fulfilled."

"How? It is so hard to forget."

"You don't have to forget. Just let go. I'm not saying forgive him. Forgiveness won't solve your trauma, only acceptance will. Accept that he was a necessary evil, a means for your ascension, nothing more. He was your trial and you passed. He is gone now. He no longer matters. It is done. He was meant to be so that you could be what you needed to be."

"I know what you are trying to, Milena. I know what you are expecting me to do. But the price… it is too high," William gave a deep sigh.

"Yes, it is. But so is the prize. Everything has a polarity to it, William. It is the law of the Allness. Everything has its counterpart. Nothing exists without its opposite. Good and evil, light and darkness, life and death. If there is one, so must be the other. This is true for life, nature and the universe alike. There must always be balance. As it is above, so it is below."

"A prize I won't live to see," said William.

"Yes, the prize will only occur if you die at that podium by the hand of a man you tried to help. This is the only chain of events that will lead to the future world you have seen. Yet, you will not live in it. You won't live to be celebrated, to be adored, to be carried on the shoulders of men. If that is what you want, you should leave all this behind and get on with your life now, try to be a rock star or something," Milena said with no hint of mockery.

"I once dreamt that; oh, how good it felt."

"Well? Tell me about it."

"Why? What does how I felt there have anything to do with what we're discussing now?"

"We are still getting to know *you*; it may be helpful," Milena said.

"All right; I kinda like this story anyway." A brief pause and he cast his mind back to that moment. "I was around thirteen and I had a rock band at high school. Shit, I could merely play the guitar. I knew no notes, no music theory, had a crappy old amp and a really bad haircut," William said with a warm smile, "But it didn't matter, I only knew one song, and that half-assed, but we applied to a talent show. Oh, boy, was that a disaster. We didn't even have a bass player."

Say your prayers little one,
Don't forget my son,
To include everyone…

His own flat voice reverberated in his head.

"This song, *Enter Sandman* was my favorite at that time. I remember the first time I heard it. I was just eleven years old and it sounded like heaven to me. It was Metallica's simplest tune but it took me more than four months to play the whole thing. Most of it was spent on the solo. Looking back, it was really basic stuff. Not for me that time though. I had goose bumps the first time I played the whole thing and it wasn't even accurate," he laughed. Milena's lovely mouth smiled back.

"You know what happened right when it was time to play the damn thing?" asked William.

"What happened?"

Her pout was adorable, like a child who doesn't know the answer to something.

William was laughing so hard, he could barely talk, like he'd just remembered a joke he hadn't heard for a long time.

"You had to secure the amp cable in the guitar's strap; that way, even if you step on it, you won't unplug it. Everyone knows that. But I didn't, no one told me. So just when I started to play the solo I'd worked on for many months, I stepped on the cable and it went off!" He carried on laughing, "And you know what the worst part is? I didn't even realize it till that solo was over. Talk about a total idiot."

Milena joined in the loud laugh. Anyone who saw them then would have been astonished to hear that William had been desolate only five minutes earlier. They laughed till it hurt.

"Oh, what a great memory! Thank you for sharing it with me, William."

"My pleasure. I'd never thought of it for many years. It was refreshing to recall that day."

"What else do you recall from that day? Other than your funny misfortune," said Milena with a smile.

"I remember how excited I was backstage. I remember eating raw eggs, six of them. I just poured them down my throat. Someone had said it would be good for my voice. It wasn't. I still sounded crap," William started to laugh again, "Oh, what an innocent day it was. Everything about that day was pure silliness and it felt magnificent."

"How did you feel on stage?"

"Like a god! Like I was on top of the world. Like I mattered."

"Do you remember the audience?" asked Milena.

"Not really. I may as well had been alone there. That's what I remember."

"And does this devalue what you'd felt there? The joy, the satisfaction?" Milena asked.

"No, it doesn't. Being there with all my heart, creating something was more than enough for me," said William in a sudden recognition.

"Which means that you didn't do it for fame or to satisfy your ego; you did it for what it meant to you. You didn't care about the applause or the cheering but the fact that you made something, you created something lasting and meaningful, for others and yourself, even if it wasn't something glorious."

"I guess, I never thought about it in this way before but you may have a point."

"And the prize is a wonderful memory that still makes you laugh and warms your heart. You worked for something day and night, made sacrifices and got your prize. It is the same for what we are dealing with here, William. The difference is the scale and the beneficiaries. What you give is what you take. This one thing we are discussing here is so big, so valuable and life changing that it demands more than hard work and sleepless nights. It demands the ultimate sacrifice. It demands *you*. You're the only thing that can tip the scales for the prize in question. This is why the price is so high. The polarity of the Allness requires it. This is the law of the Allness," Milena said.

"What do you mean by the law of the Allness? Second time you mention it."

"It is *the* law. The law of all existence. It is hard to comprehend when you are trapped in a material shell. But simply put, it means that in all its vastness and infinity, everything that is and has been, in fact, is one. Don't ponder, you're not ready yet. The one thing you need to understand and accept about the Allness is that it, the universal law, is founded on polarity. The scales must always be balanced. Every prize has its own price," she explained.

"I understand. But still, there is a choice to be made."

"There is, William… Always. Nothing is written in stone. What you choose is what you get. People rarely see far enough to grasp the consequences of their actions. And when they do, they usually get it wrong. It also depends on their intentions. Self-serving intentions do not bring the desired results, because they are not righteous, therefore not pure. The Allness can see it and reject their wishes. Only selfless and pure intentions cause the intended results to manifest themselves. False humility, false compassion, false kindness for self-serving ends never justify themselves. The Allness can see through them like glass. Remember your innocent prayers. You wanted love, affection, you wanted something pure and righteous and you made it real. This is what I mean by intentions," Milena said.

"So even if I choose to walk this path, I should do so with selfless intentions, so dying for it isn't enough, I must also be righteous and sincere in it?"

"I'm afraid so," Milena said.

"You ask for too much…".

"It's not me who asks for it, William; it is the law," Milena said.

"You don't expect me to explain this Allness to my people, do you? I'm not sure they would understand, let alone take me seriously. It would sound like new age mumbo-jumbo to them."

"The Allness is for you, William. For you to know and try to understand, so you can put meaning to your choices and your actions. People of your time are not yet conscious or learned enough to conceive this concept. You only need to make them aware that they must change their perception of good and evil, right and wrong. They must first learn to be righteous and live with higher virtues. In time, the new way will lead them to expand their minds and ascend them to a level where the Allness will not just be understood but embraced. So don't worry, this will be someone else's challenge," Milena replied.

William kept silent for a minute. He delved into his thoughts like he was searching for something deep down. His gaze was transfixed on something that was not there. His mouth moved up and down perplexedly. Then he said:

"You know what the only reason holding me back is, right? Since you can read my thoughts."

"They'll be fine, William, trust me. But this is not your main concern. It comes second to your own selfish desire. Not that it is evil but selfish nonetheless."

"I love them, more than myself, more than this shitty world and everything in it. I can't bear the thought of not seeing them grow or hug them anymore," William confessed.

"You're only human, William, I understand. But who said you wouldn't see them again?"

"You mean the afterlife?"

"No, William, the afterlife is a concept you invented. There is no before or after. There is here, the material world and there, the end destination where you reunite with the Allness. The thing you fear most is inevitable. Three years from now or a hundred years later: it makes no difference in an eternity of the Allness. It is nothing but a blink. A mere split-second delay. Know that everything you fear is the result of your thoughts, your own imagination, nothing more. Everyone and everything are bound to unite in the Allness, sooner or later," Milena said.

William raised his eyes at the sky. Looking at the vastness of space, he realized he could only catch a glimpse of it and felt lost trying to visualize the whole. He imagined one of the stars he was seeing had already been dead for millions of years; it no longer existed. It was an unfathomable idea. How could something not even be real if he could see it with his own eyes? What was reality then? Was it the eyes that see or the mind that creates? What was this Allness? How did it come to be? Who made it? Who made the one that made the Allness? He had so many questions, there were so many unknowns. Even so, they converged into one:

"How will I leave my kids willingly?"

"How long do I have to decide?" he asked Milena.

"You already did, William and you know it. You're just still afraid to admit it to yourself," Milena said, her hands on William's cheeks now. For a moment, he thought she would kiss him. Then he remembered that it would not happen for another three years. A single tear born out of his left eye fell down his cheek. Milena's long, smooth fingers wiped it away.

"How do I start; where do I begin? Will you be with me along the way? I don't know how to do it; I feel lost more than ever. I need you by my side," William said in a shaky voice.

"You have everything you need. You will find your way, trust me. You do not need me anymore. You don't need anybody. All you need is already within you. My task is done; you won't see me for another three years, William. And you will do so only if you choose."

Choice. A word that both pleased and terrified him.

"Let's walk to your house. It's nearly seven o'clock. You don't want to miss spaghetti night, do you?" asked Milena.

William found it both hilarious and surprising that *spaghetti* was the word to bring him back to the present, like a keyword waking him up from a deep hypnosis. He smiled at Milena.

"That would be nice."

They set off along the river and carried on down the streets. It took forty-five minutes. William cherished every second of it. They both kept silent all that time, communicating every once in a while as their eyes met. Everything that had to be said was said. No more words were needed.

As they reached the gate, a terrible sadness filled William's heart. He remembered it at once. It was the same feeling when he had to say goodbye to Rachel every Sunday night until the following Friday, when they were still only lovers and he went to college in another city. It was the melancholy heartbreak of parting.

But this was much more intense; he knew he wouldn't see Milena for another three years, and even then, only for a short moment. A long time to wait for a single, brief kiss.

Despite the sorrow, he felt alive again.

"How do we say goodbye?" he asked.

"We don't. There is never a goodbye. We will be together again, as will all things. You and I are bound now; we will find each other," said Milena, "But before I go, I have one last gift for you, Pups."

She took a few steps back and stood directly in front of William. She bowed her head. Her blazing tresses obscured her face. Then she slowly lifted her head again. As her hair fell to her wide shoulders, William found himself looking at a brightly shining face with faintly visible features. It was like the sun shone out of her body in all its glory. Her yellow eyes were now transformed into sparklers. William was enraptured by the energy emanating from that ethereal being.

A faint fear paid his heart a momentary visit. It passed in a mere instant. It made no difference to his affection for this creature, whatever she or it was.

"What are you really?" asked William, fascinated.

"Does it matter to you if I'm this or that?" she asked in a euphonious voice.

"No. It does not. Not anymore. I accept you as you are. Whatever you are, first and foremost, you are my precious now," replied William in a gentle, affectionate tone. This was no compliment or flattery. He fully meant it. He knew the time to part with her was just minutes ahead. Longing enveloped his heart. An envelope that would only be ripped open on reunion with her.

As he wrestled with his melancholy, Milena reached down into her glowing bare chest and pulled out the biggest, shiniest red apple William had ever seen. She held it up to her face and gazed at it. Then, throwing it to William, she said:

"You deserve it. Know that I love you with all my heart... "

And before he could reply, she vanished into thin air, just the way she had first appeared.

William watched the space she left behind with tearful, yet eyes sparkling. He wanted to say, "I love you too" before she left. He said it anyway to that now vacant space, like she was still there. It gave him a sense of closure.

Next, he gazed at the apple he was gripping tight, lifted it to his mouth without a blink and took a bite.

A wonderful explosion of light and sparklers filled his vision. Everything that has been and ever will be flashed before his eyes in a millisecond. The first particles, the first chaos, the first light of the first star, the first supernova, and the carbon atoms it spewed out to seed the planets with life, the beautiful, wild dance of the galaxies around black holes and everything that followed.

He, who was not the same man before his journey with Milena, was yet another man after that bite.

Then it stopped.

He stood there like a statue for a few minutes. Then a silly smile spread on his face. He turned back and opened the gate. Walking up to the front door slowly, he rang the bell. Light steps hurried toward him.

Candice opened the door.

"Daddy!" she jumped and hugged him as tight as she could. So did William.

"Daddy, it's spaghetti night! You're late," she said cheerfully.

"I know honey, I'm sorry… I'm here now. Come on, let's go in and eat."

He walked in, still carrying his daughter. Made straight for the dining room to be greeted by Rachel and Charlie's eyes shining with love.

One single thought crossed his mind.

What a world.

THE END

Made in the USA
Monee, IL
18 August 2022